DEATH OF A CON MAN

A car accident, a passenger who disappears and a
knife that turns up suggest certain lines of inquiry
to the police, but when the young doctor on out-
patients discovers the dying driver's blood group details
have been altered in his pocket diary, it is too
late to save a life, but puts a different complexion
on the case. Setting out to clear his colleague's
name, Dr Colin Frost finds himself involved in a
history of sordid small-time intrigue which suddenly
erupts into savage violence.

Death of a Con Man

JOSEPHINE BELL

HODDER AND STOUGHTON

Copyright © 1968 Doris Ball
SBN 340 02912 9
First printed 1968

Printed in Great Britain for Hodder and Stoughton Limited,
St. Paul's House, Warwick Lane, London, E.C.4, by
Northumberland Press Limited, Gateshead

CHAPTER ONE

The man was very well known. To the police, that is. Though not to the local force.

The crash occurred about five miles from the Wiltshire town of Brackenfield that lies between Salisbury Plain and the outskirts of the New Forest. At a sharp bend in the three-lane road, on a late evening in October, with a light mist swirling from wet ditches across the tarmac, a coach bringing a charter party back from a conference in Plymouth met head-on a black Hillman that had taken the sharp bend too fast and failed to get round it.

Apart from the mist patches, which were low lying, confusing, but not really dangerous, conditions were easy, the road dry, a clear night above, but no moon. The whole fault lay with the driver of the Hillman. It was he, except for the wrecked car, who suffered the only severe damage.

The driver of the coach had about two seconds in which to decide that the Hillman was not going to get round the bend. He swung the coach over, so it was his offside wing and the offside corner of the coach that took the crunch. The same with the Hillman, including the driver, who in spite of his safety belt, which broke, had his right arm pierced and lacerated by several long splinters of glass from his side window. He was also knocked out but not seriously concussed by the crumpled window frame striking him on the head.

The coach driver, though severely shaken, at once switched off his engine, which had stalled, and sliding across from behind the wheel climbed down on the near side into two feet of ditch water where he expected the margin of the road to be.

The cold shock to his feet and legs cleared his dazed mind. He splashed on to firm ground further back and opening the rear door and the emergency exit, both quite unaffected by the crash, began to sort out the mass of struggling, screaming or stunned passengers.

Two men, sitting at the rear of the coach, had, however, kept their heads. One leaped down at once volunteering to stop the next arriving car behind and all subsequent cars. He feared a pile-up. The driver agreed. The second man had a pocket torch. He proposed to move forward to deal with traffic from the other side.

The driver then forced his way into the coach to quell the hysteria that had taken hold there and to sort out any injured passengers. Guided by his own escape, he did not expect to find anything serious, nor did he. A fair proportion of genuine shock, much hysteria, simulating shock, a few cuts. Most of his passengers had no idea what had happened. In explaining the accident to them it occurred to him for the first time to wonder what had happened to the driver of the car that had hit the coach. And the car's passengers, if any.

Cursing to himself at the thought of what he might find, he left the coach again, followed now by all those who felt sufficiently restored to be both curious and in need of fresh air.

The driver saw at once that the sensible man who had first offered help had the tail queue under control and was already discussing the situation with the drivers of the first four cars in the line. So the coachdriver made his way cautiously forward to where the smashed car lay slewed across the road. There was room for an ordinary car to pass it, but the first to arrive from the direction of Brackenfield had been a tall removal van that could not get through. The crew of this van was clustered together on the far side of the remains of the Hillman. The coach passenger with the torch was shining it past them into the car.

"Dead?" asked the coach driver, bitterly, feeling this fate would be nothing but an unfair escape from a juster punishment.

"Not yet," said the van driver. "Pretty poor shape, though. Arm mucked up by glass. Lost a couple of pints, I reckon. 'Fore I got a tourniquet on."

"You a medico or something?" asked the coach driver, trying to peer in at the casualty, but without much success.

"Picked it up in the war," said one of the van's crew. "Knows 'is stuff all right."

"Can't we get him out of there?" the coach driver asked, nervously. He had got one glimpse of a set white face with closed eyes, the head lolled over against the left shoulder, a stained and spattered shirt, legs limp and twisted, an arm bandaged tightly above the elbow, but below that a mass of torn cloth, flesh and clotting blood.

The man with the torch said, "I got the first car behind the van to turn and go back to phone. He'd have to find another way round, anyhow. We ought to have an ambulance and the police before long. Listen! Isn't that them?"

Sirens were wailing from both directions. The meaning of this became plain in a few seconds. The police had already diverted traffic leaving Brackenfield and were now peeling cars off the outgoing stream, to find their own way round along the side roads. This done, a police car arrived behind the van, to move it back enough to allow the ambulance that had driven round to arrive from the opposite direction, to mount the verge, squeeze past and draw up behind the smashed Hillman.

"Quick work," said the man with the torch admiringly.

The police sergeant paid no attention to this, but asked what the damage was.

"Casualties?" he said briskly, nodding to the two ambulance men, who had just left their vehicle.

"One serious," said the coach driver. "The lunatic who put his Hillman where you see it."

"None in your coach?" asked the sergeant.

The ambulance driver went back to unload a stretcher and blankets. The other man looked into the Hillman, nodding with pleasure at sight of the improvised tourniquet.

"Glass, I reckon," said the van driver. "Fair split his arm—talk about bacon machines—"

"Belt up!" said one of his crew, retching audibly.

The ambulance man felt for the pulse at the other wrist, failed to find it, but found a faint movement in the neck. With the help of the ex-soldier the two St John men got the limp form out and lowered it carefully on to the stretcher.

While this was being done the police sergeant took a brief statement from the coach driver.

"Casualties?" he repeated. The cause of the accident was entirely obvious.

"A good few bruises and slight cuts. Shock, naturally."

Voices from the coach, raised partly in anger, partly in distress, confirmed this view. The sergeant made up his mind.

"If we get the Hillman away from your wing, can you drive the coach into Brackenfield?" he asked.

"Don't know as I can."

"Well, see if you've got your engine. There's enough help here to clear you."

The coach engine responded. The furniture van crew produced useful slings and jacks. The coach backed away from the ditch, many willing hands hauled the wreck from its path and it drove slowly forward.

"Take them all straight to the hospital," the sergeant ordered. "You can ring your firm from there. O.K.?"

"O.K.," said the driver, sullenly. He saw hours of trouble ahead, if not today, certainly tomorrow. Not to speak of forms to fill, arguments with the boss, the insurance, perhaps the coroner. Yes, almost certainly the coroner. The nut in the Hillman was for the high jump all right.

Meanwhile the ambulance had gone, tearing through the night, through the thinning mist, through the lighted outskirts of Brackenfield, its two-note siren screaming all the way. People left their tellies to peer from their windows at the cream-coloured monster with its revolving blue light on top, rushing past. Then went back, grumbling because the distraction had been unrewarding. But the noise and the speed were justified, for the casualty was not dead; desperately ill from loss of blood and consequent shock, but recovered enough from the blow on his head to whisper to the St John driver as the stretcher went up into the ambulance, "Blood group. In my diary. Blood group."

"What's he say?" asked the other man.

"Something about his blood group. Knows what he needs, don't he? In his diary, he says."

"O.K. Get started, Tom. I'll see to it. Fast as you can. He's off again, isn't he?"

"That's right."

"Flat out, poor sod. Don't like the look of him at all."

Nor did the driver. But while there was life ... he said to himself, repeating it in his mind, as he always did on these occasions. The motto had brought him into the ambulance service when his air-raid warden's job came to an end. It had turned him into an air-raid warden when he was a medically rejected army recruit in the third year of the war. In the ambulance he now drove there was a life hanging by a thread. With this and other favourite clichés helping his concentration he covered the five miles to Brackenfield in record time and the mile and a half through the still crowded main streets to the new Casualty department of the town's ancient general hospital in less than five minutes more.

Meanwhile the second man, tending the casualty inside the ambulance, improved the rough but efficient first aid given by the crew of the furniture van and then began gently feeling in the casualty's pockets for the diary.

He found it fairly soon. As the injured man continued unconscious and his colour did not improve, while his breathing became rather more rapid, his attendant gave all his attention to the book, since immediate transfusion seemed to offer the only chance to repel death until the man's injuries could be properly treated.

Fortunately the little diary he had found was the right one.

On the first page, following the name, James Sparks, and a line for the address, not filled in, there were various headings for age, measurements, insurance details, telephone number and so on. These too were blank. Below, at the foot of the page, there was a heading written in ink, not printed, stating blood group and giving the information. A quick run through the pages confirmed that this was the only entry of its kind.

The ambulance man glanced once more at the casualty. Still out cold. Perhaps a little colder, in spite of the blankets and the heater. Perhaps a little further down the slippery slope. But the pulse in the neck still beat. Casualty department, not to mortuary.

A few seconds later the ambulance swung through the wide gates of the hospital, past the main entrance and steps, round the corner of the building into a wide bay. Here the driver backed to the door of Casualty and stopped.

On the main road, though the diversion still operated, the police were now alone with the wrecked car. While his driver sorted out and disposed of the furniture van and the held-up cars, the sergeant, returning to the police car, got in touch with headquarters in Brackenfield. He gave a brief account of the accident, reported that one very serious, and several minor casualties had now proceeded to the hospital, where evidence could be taken from the coach driver and his passengers. He asked that a breakdown van be sent to collect the wrecked car. It could not be left on the road. Apart from the large quantity of broken glass, there was a considerable amount of blood. In fact the shambles had to be seen to be believed, the sergeant said, with only one serious casualty.

When he went back to the Hillman he found his driver in a state of some excitement. The latter had got rid of all the waiting cars and had set out accident warning lights at either end of the curve in the road to warn the breakdown van and any car that had missed the diversion. Having done this he had taken a look at the inside of the wreck and had discovered two surprising facts.

"What's up?" asked the sergeant, arriving behind the other's broad back, which showed no sign of moving.

"He had a bird with him—by all appearances."

"They thought he might. Found something?"

"The seat belt's had an almighty jerk, broken in two places, but it kept him off the wheel. And there's a lipstick at the edge of the carpet on the passenger side and a lady's handkerchief on the floor at the back. Stained with blood. See for yourself."

He heaved himself away to let the sergeant take his place.

"You're right," the latter agreed softly. "Now why the blazes—?"

"If there was a bird in there with the chap, where's she vanished to?" asked the constable.

"Search me. Better have a look round. They wander off sometimes, dazed, don't they?"

"She can't have gone far."

"You never know."

"With him in the state he was, it'd be a miracle— Hullo, 'ullo, 'ullo!"

"Well?"

"I just kicked it. Ruddy great—well, no, not so big, really."

The constable was now shining his torch down on to the grass beside the ditch. A knife lay there, a boy's knife, a scout's knife, with a strong blade and a curved bone handle. The sergeant wrapped his handkerchief round it and picked it up very carefully.

"Another inch and it'd been in the water," he said, reproachfully.

"Where it was meant to be," said the constable.

The two men looked at each other. The sergeant unwrapped the knife again while the constable shone his torch on it.

"Blood," they said together.

"And we thought it all came from that torn arm," said the sergeant slowly. "It's the car, all right. I should think it must be *him!*"

He made a sudden dash back to the police car and the

constable heard him calling the station again. It was a long
conversation, or so it seemed to the other standing guard over
the wreck. Before it was finished the breakdown van arrived
from the direction of Brackenfield. The constable explained
the accident to the two men who got out of it. They all walked
round the Hillman, but the constable would not let the new
arrivals touch the doors or look at the inside. In a few seconds
the sergeant joined them.

"We want this lot at the station," he said, crisply. "There's
quite a few things we have to check."

"Whatever you say, mate," answered the driver of the
breakdown van. He had nothing against the Law, but he was
always on his guard against self-importance in a uniform,
whoever it might be, from a cinema commissionaire upwards.

"Get cracking, then," said the sergeant coldly.

In the police car, following the van to make sure its in-
dependent-minded driver developed no independent ideas of
personal investigation, the sergeant remarked, "They're going
up to the hospital to see if the chap has a stab wound."

"Hope it's useful," answered the constable, who was bored
with driving so slowly.

"They think it is him."

"Who? The hospital? They should. He'd have something on
him. Wallet or something."

"Name, James Sparks at the moment. But when he was last
booked and sent down for two years he was Fred Holmes.
Quite an old pal, it seems."

"You don't say. What's his lay? Breaking?"

"Oh, no. Conning. Female nuts. Soaks up their savings like a
sponge. Been inside twice. Usually known now as Flash Jim."

The constable was so astonished he nearly ran into the tail
of the wrecked Hillman, as the breakdown van drew up at the
first traffic lights of the town.

"D'you mean to say the Super rustled all that up in the time
between you first got them and the second, after we found the
knife?"

"Be your age! No, we didn't know him here. But the Super had a general call for Jim Sparks, alias Fred Holmes. Left the nick, having done his last stretch, just over a month ago. Got a job at Gregson's dive here. Knows one of Greg's girls. Hasn't been seen in London since his last conviction. Now we have a stolen car to locate, together with a missing barman and club hostess. Car was the Hillman, for sure. Hadn't had time to change the number. Rest ties in, doesn't it?"

"Should do. Wonder where he was going?"

"We may know that very soon. Where we can't follow."

The police station came in view ahead, the gates to its yard wide open, with a uniformed constable beside them.

"Do the necessary and get rid of these chaps," the sergeant said. "I'll nip in and take them the knife. Don't let anyone touch the inside or out. Tell them we'll be after their finger-prints if they do."

The sergeant disappeared into the station. The constable parked the police car behind the wreck. The two men lowered the smashed front of it, released their crane and prepared to go. Any curiosity they may have had was gone, evaporated in the cold night air. They wanted to get back to the warm stuffy office at their garage. If there was another emergency call, it would be just too bad.

The constable saw them out of the yard. The man at the gates shut and locked them. Then both men went inside.

In the corridor they met the patrol sergeant coming away from the superintendent's room. He stopped when he saw them.

"Super wants you, Ron," he said to the constable who had been at the yard gates. "About that emergency call to this accident. The first one."

"The woman who ordered us to send an ambulance right away?"

"That's right. Didn't leave a name or address, did she?"

"No. The next one did, man who'd come back in his car to report. Thing is, he'd slowed down at the first telephone call box near the road, not far from the bend, near a group of cottages, seen a woman in it nattering away and thought it was quicker to drive on."

'That's right. So he probably saw the woman we want."

"You mean the one who phoned?"

"Who knows a lot we'd like to have from her."

"Probably stuck the poor chap herself and then panicked," said the patrol constable. "Is he still alive?"

"They don't hold out much hopes," said the sergeant.

"Whoever said they would."

On the road from Brackenfield no trace of the accident remained but a scuffed surface of the road, an oil patch, a shower of glass and a lingering scent of petrol in the air.

The mist still hung a few feet from the ground, though above it the night was clear, with stars. A low, late, gibbous moon had now appeared above the trees at the other side of a bordering field. Its pale light shone on the dark figure of a man who, in the intervals between passing cars, when he bent to hide himself against the hedge, searched and searched again the water of the ditch and the verge of grass for the knife that was no longer there.

At last, cursing bitterly both his failure and the cold wetness of his legs and arms, he climbed back into the field where he had lain in hiding, crossed it and the next one and travelling on by cross-country paths and lanes, reached Brackenfield and his lodgings there in safety and, as far as he knew, unrecognised by any living soul.

CHAPTER TWO

When the ambulance drew up at the Casualty doors of the hospital, Joe Gibson, the attendant, hurried inside. On the chairs for waiting patients he saw the usual small late evening crowd, the inevitable ton-up boys in studded leather jackets surrounding their companion who had failed to take a corner and took a toss instead. The injured lad, so well padded and helmeted that his injuries were slight, was making the most of his mishap, drowning his humiliation in groans and obscenities that brought indignant stares from the other sufferers and a sharp rebuke from the nurse at reception.

"Stop that or out you go, ankle and all! No filth in here, my lad!"

A chorus of indignation assailed her.

"Wot if it's broke? Got to 'ave X-ray, ain't 'e?"

"That's for the doctor to say. Now will you all keep quiet, or do I get the porter to see to you? Remember some people here really are ill."

Joe pushed past the boys, now muttering in low voices, the mother with the gangling son who had cut his hand with a tin opener, the parents whose burnt child was howling in a cubicle beyond the waiting room.

"Urgent case, Nurse," he said. "Road accident. Haemorrhage Bringing him in now."

The nurse reached for the phone on her desk to call the registrar on duty. At the same time she said quickly, "Dr Patel's in with that child."

She turned to the phone. Joe hurried forward, through the swing doors into the treatment room. In the nearest cubicle the doctor was dressing the child's burn, helped by a student nurse. He listened to Joe, told the nurse to finish the bandaging and hurried out of the cubicle, followed by Joe, who held out the diary to him. They met the trolley with the stretcher on it, pushed by the night porter and the St John driver. The nurse in reception was just behind. Minor cases could wait.

"Doctor," Joe urged. "This was in his pocket. Gives his blood group. Look. Here."

But Patel had followed the stretcher. He had brought forward the necessary apparatus to take a specimen of blood for matching. He worked quickly and accurately.

"Great loss of blood," he said, more to himself than the others. "Transfusion will be needed. Do not move the patient. Immediate—"

"Look, Doctor!" Joe was at Patel's side, insistent. "His blood group. Marked up in his diary. Save time, wouldn't it?"

"What do you say?" The dark Indian face, frozen in concentration, in anxiety to start the correct treatment as soon as possible, frowned as its owner understood what he had just heard.

"You have the blood?"

"The group. Written here. Look."

Dr Patel looked, understood, realised that time, precious time, might be saved. He glanced at the figure on the stretcher, at the nurse. Hesitated, but not for more than a second. Because with a swish of the cubicle curtain night staff nurse was there, ordering the right emergency trolley, which the nurse ran to fetch, directing the porter, the St John driver; herself bringing forward the oxygen cylinder with one hand and getting out her scissors with the other.

Dr Patel made up his mind. Time would indeed be saved. He ran to the desk at the side of the room opposite the cubicle. He propped the diary on it, copied the particulars on to a patient's case sheet, copied the blood group letters again on to a piece of paper and hurried away.

He was back from the laboratory in less than three minutes, meeting the registrar, Colin Frost, at the inner door of Casualty.

"I have blood for urgent case," he said and continued to explain volubly as he hurried behind Colin to the cubicle where staff nurse was actively engaged in preparing the patient for treatment.

"Road accident, is he, Staff?" Colin said, when he had the transfusion going and found time to speak. "Not the only one, surely?"

The staff nurse shook her head.

"There's a bus load outside. Reception wouldn't let them all in, but there's about twenty asking for treatment and with their friends and relations—"

She broke off to look outside the cubicle and through the half-glassed wall at the waiting area, where the nurse on duty was trying to induce order out of very persistent chaos.

"Go and read the riot act to them, Patty," Colin said to the Indian, who had been assisting him. "We've done what we can here for the moment."

As the houseman went away, not very sure what he was supposed to do, staff nurse said in a worried voice, "I can't think why that silly girl hasn't come back."

"What silly girl?"

"The student nurse I sent for the blood."

"But Dr Patel gave me the blood. He'd just been for it."

"How did he know—?"

"Chap's diary. Group written in it. Thought he'd save time."

"I don't understand," said the nurse. "I don't know what you're talking about."

"Nor do I, really," Colin confessed. "I simply met him in the corridor with the stuff and he told me he'd got the group from the casualty's diary."

"I sent the student nurse in the ordinary way," staff nurse replied angrily. "Dr Patel should have told me. I saw him take the specimen. I sent the girl with it at once."

"He thought he was saving time," said Colin. "Not that it looks as if it much mattered."

For the injured man showed no sign of improvement, though he still lived.

"I'll have a word with Patty," the registrar said. "You hold the fort, Staff. Send the girl out to me when she comes back. We're sure to need her lot of blood, too."

When he opened the door into the waiting room the noise there seemed deafening. But at his appearance it dropped suddenly to a murmur.

He knew why. He was in charge of the principal casualty. They all guessed that and hoped for a dramatic announcement. So he looked round slowly, nodded to Patel, who, almost submerged, was evidently trying to get histories of injury from half a dozen vociferous minor sufferers. He turned his head away again to where the uniformed figures of the St John ambulance men were urging the coach driver to get his un-injured passengers back into the coach.

Colin went up to this group.

"Which of you told Dr Patel about a diary with a blood group in it?" he asked.

They all swung round to face him.

"I 'ad nothing to do with the nut that hit me," the coach driver said. "Occupied with my passengers. Proper shake-up, it was."

The St John driver interrupted.

"Fellow came round as we were lowering him to the stretcher," he said. "Told me, 'Blood group. Diary. Blood group.' Just those words. Very faint, but clear. My mate found it, didn't you, Joe?"

"That's right," the other man agreed. "In his pocket. After I'd made sure the arm was properly fixed. I ran in here with it as quick as I could and gave it the dark doctor over there."

"Thank you."

Colin looked round again.

"You needn't wait," he said. "We'll be admitting your case. No one else by the look of it, but I'll make sure."

"Excuse me, sir," the St John man said, quiet but insistent. "We were waiting to collect our stretcher. And the blankets."

Colin flushed. He was still young enough to overlook pro-tocol in cases of emergency.

"Go in and get it," he said. "That is if staff nurse will let you. If not, come and get me."

He moved away to help Patel, who had at last managed to sort out three definite cases for treatment and four more potential ones.

"Now then," he said. "It's time you people went home. Your driver isn't complaining and he got the worst of the smash. Dr

Patel will look after the bruises and little cuts. The rest of you don't need hospital treatment. Bed with a couple of aspirins. See your own doctors in the morning if necessary. Off you go."

A murmur went up. Several indignant voices began to mutter. In exasperation Colin turned his back on the crowd. At that moment a nasal whine came from the ton-up boys, who had been overwhelmed and totally neglected when the coach invasion flooded the waiting room.

" 'Oo does 'e think 'e is? 'E can't speak to us like that. Treatment, that's wot we're 'ere for."

The cry was taken up.

"Treatment! That wot we're 'ere for!"

Colin swung round again, prepared to do battle if it came to that. Patel's face took on a greenish tinge.

But allies were at hand. Through the outside door came two mackintoshed figures, at sight of whom the leather-coated boys melted away to the back of the waiting room. And from the door of the treatment room the night sister on duty stepped forward, blue-cloaked, immaculate, her grey curls framing her pleated muslin cap.

"You've all heard what Mr Frost said," she announced, crisply, "so be sensible and go back to your coach and let the driver take you home. *All* of you," she added, looking coldly at the small group segregated by Patel. "You are not suffering from shock now, that's very evident. Are they, Dr Patel?"

"No, Sister," he said. "They do not suffer anything but excitement."

A few of the more robust spirits laughed. Others followed.

"You can see your own doctors in the morning," Sister encouraged them.

"I'm not staying to be insulted by *him*," one stout woman announced. "Disgraceful! Call theirselves doctors!"

"I've a good mind to make a complaint," added another.

But the two were ignored. The rest had realised suddenly that they were tired, cold, hungry, and above all thirsty. After hours, too. Pubs all shut by now. Or were they? To their enormous surprise they saw by the clock on the wall that it was barely ten.

"Time for a quick one," someone called. In a couple of minutes the waiting hall was empty.

The mackintoshed detective-constable held the door open as they passed through. Then he closed the door and stood away from it. He had seen the boys go out but had not spoken to them, though he knew them well. He smiled as he noticed one of them limping slightly. Teach the young tearaway to ride more carefully, perhaps. If he still had the bike when it was mended. If it was his own, not stolen.

After Sister had spoken, Colin moved away, going back into the treatment room. He had been out of it only five minutes, but in that time the casualty's state had changed alarmingly. Staff nurse was very worried.

"He's just had what looked like a rigor," she said.

Colin felt for the man's pulse. It had returned at the wrist, so he should be showing some improvement, not this intense blue colour, this harsh, rapid shallow breathing.

The registrar saw that the two ambulance men were inside the cubicle, waiting patiently to remove their gear.

"Lift him for me," he said, beckoning to them for help. "There must be more here than we've seen already. He ought to be picking up. I don't understand—"

With expert ease the two did as he asked, sliding out the poles and canvas of the stretcher at the same time and slipping away their own blankets as the nurse spread hospital ones instead.

It was now quite clear that the lacerated arm had not been the only source of the injured man's haemorrhage and collapse. A clean slit in jacket and shirt at the back over the left side of the chest showed through a stiffening area of blood. The wound was a couple of inches long and had gone deep. While the victim was still sitting in the car it must have bled copiously, pouring down his back to the waist. On the stretcher his own weight had put pressure on it enough to stop

the outward flow. This new movement, careful and restricted
as it was, started it again.

"Pad!" said Colin, quickly. "Strapping!"

Staff nurse thrust the oxygen mask into the hands of the
student nurse, who had returned from the lab, and stooped to
the trolley to supply Colin. He secured the wound with strapping as a temporary measure and they turned the man gently
on to his back again.

"That came from the other side and behind," Colin said,
more puzzled than ever. "That wasn't from windscreen glass
or window glass or whatever messed up his arm."

"No," said a quiet voice behind him. "If I'm not mistaken it
came from a knife."

The registrar turned quickly. Just inside the curtains of the
cubicle were the two mackintoshed figures that had arrived at
the moment of crisis in the waiting room.

"Detective-Inspector Rawlinson," said the older of the two,
stepping forward. "A knife has been picked up at the scene of
the accident by the patrol who have been dealing with it on
the road. Would you say that injury you've just discovered is a
knife wound?"

"I'd say it was an incised wound," said Colin, exasperated by
this added complication. "I'm not prepared to say how he got
it. Will you please wait outside. The patient is desperately ill
and we can't allow you in here while we're working on him."

"Not if I tell you he is someone we have been asked to find
and who may help us in certain inquiries?"

"He can't help you at the moment and he doesn't look like
helping you in the future," said Colin. "Patty, take them outside and see if you can get any sense out of them."

"I'm sorry you should take this tone, Doctor," said the inspector, considerably affronted by Colin's indifference to the
needs of the law.

"Look," said Colin. "I'm trying to save a man's life and I don't
care if he's a spy or a great train robber or a defaulting
millionaire or just a poor bloody lunatic who drives his car

into a coach. You're in my way and what I say here and now goes. So—out."

"His name is James Sparks," said Patel, trying to help both sides at once in this alarming encounter. "I have his diary. At the desk. Follow me. I show you. Name and, providentially, blood group."

"Blood group!"

A warning light shone in Colin's brain. He looked round quickly. On the trolley stood the supply the student nurse had brought from the laboratory. Attached to the patient was the drip from the supply brought by Ahmed Patel, whom he had met with it in the corridor. Staff nurse said, "Dr Patel went off at once to get it. He had the diary with the group noted in it, you said."

"But he didn't check with the man's blood?"

She shook her head.

"I don't know. He took the specimen so I thought he must have, but perhaps not. I came in just as he was leaving to get the blood. It was very urgent."

"And you?"

"I told you. I thought we'd need more so I sent Nurse Ray here along. The usual routine."

Colin picked up the second supply. It was clearly marked. He went back to the first. A small difference; a subtle difference; but lethal.

Patel was searching the desk with frantic gestures when Colin pushed past the two police officers to join him.

"That diary!" he demanded, in a low urgent voice.

"I look for it!" Patel answered, despairingly. "These—officers need it. I explain I leave it here on the desk on the notes I make for the casualty. Here—the notes. No diary."

Inspector Rawlinson said heavily, "Was it possible for the case at the material time to leave the cubicle and return to it with his diary?"

"Leave the cubicle! Good God, man, haven't you seen him?"

Rawlinson controlled his temper with a considerable effort.

"I saw him just now," he said, "when he certainly appeared too ill to move on his own. I have no knowledge of his condition on arrival. This doctor explains that he was given a diary by one of the ambulance men and that Jim—I mean your patient—had said in the ambulance his blood group was written in the diary."

"It was so written," Patel insisted, his own voice rising. "I saw it. I had it in my hand. I copied the letters of the group. Here. You see on his form."

Colin stooped to verify them with those he had read in the cubicle. The inspector, having already done this, stood stiffly waiting.

"Quite right," Colin said. "You made a note here and that was the stuff you fetched. You took a specimen to the lab. Was that the bottle the technician there gave you?"

"No. Because I had this. I took a bottle myself." Patel frowned. He could not see the point of all these questions. "I save time," he said. "Information to hand. I act at once."

"It isn't to hand any longer," Inspector Rawlinson said.

But his remark was lost on Colin, who was already back in the cubicle, where the nurse had, at his order, dismantled the drip, fixed in the fresh supply of compatible blood, laid aside the other.

"Don't let anyone touch a thing, Staff," he ordered. "Keep on as you are. I've got to phone."

The situation was beyond him, he realised. The diary, wherever it was now, had lied. Its lying information had been recorded, but had not been checked either by the Indian or by himself. The damage was done. Could it be repaired? That was what he had to know. And what must now be done?

The consultant was understanding, but cold. He gave instructions. Said he would come to the hospital at once. Rang off.

Back in Casualty Colin did everything he had been told, helped by a shivering, tearful Patel, an icily indignant night sister and two silent nurses. The police officers, provided now with chairs, sat outside the cubicle. Twice Inspector Rawlinson tiptoed out to reception to phone police head-quarters, the first time to make a report about the injured man, the second to announce the arrival of the consultant.

The losing battle continued for another three hours, until at two in the morning the victim of his own folly, another's murderous assault and the inexperienced urge to succour of a third, gave up the struggle to live and was pronounced dead.

The consultant, gravely concerned, spoke to Inspector Rawlinson.

"Gone, poor chap," he said to him. "I understand you had a professional interest."

"A very old friend of the law," said the inspector, regret-fully.

"Enemy, don't you mean?" said the consultant. "Who fin-ally has got away from you."

"Yes, sir. Just as well for him, I daresay." Rawlinson stopped himself explaining further, but added, "Can you give me the cause of death, sir?"

The consultant said smoothly, without hesitation, "The cause of death was a road accident. The medical detail will be produced at the inquest, of course."

"Quite so, sir," the inspector answered.

The consultant was turning away when a new voice behind him made him look back. A smaller, thinner figure, in spectacles, with a pinched eager look on his bony face, had emerged from behind the heavy figures of the two detectives.

"What about the diary, sir?" the new man said. "The Ind—the dark doctor said it was most important. Terribly, horribly important, his words to me were. And they can't find it."

"Are you a journalist?" asked the consultant, angry now, showing it deliberately.

"Well—well, yes. I—"

"Then you have no business to be in this room. Leave it at once. And the hospital. At once."

"But, Doctor—"

"If your editor wants information he may ring up the hospital secretary in the morning. Before nine, if he expects to get him personally. Goodnight to you."

His words were addressed to all three men. The police officers moved away, sweeping the still protesting journalist with them. The nurse in reception put out some of the lights there and settled down to sorting out and filing her case notes for the evening.

In the treatment room the consultant spoke to Colin before he too left the hospital.

"Looks as if you'll have to get the police on to finding his next of kin," he said. "Bad business, all round."

He glanced across at Ahmed Patel, who was, yet once more, searching behind and round the desk for the lost diary.

"He swears he copied the group from the diary," Colin said, unhappily. "It's not the sort of thing anyone would invent."

"It's the sort of thing that type would invent if he'd rushed off to the lab for blood and arrived without a clue, so said the first thing he thought of to save face."

"I don't believe for a moment Patty would do that!" Colin protested. "Besides I know he did take a specimen from the man. He just didn't wait for it to be matched because he thought he had the answer."

The Indian, though he could not hear what they said, understood from their frequent glances in his direction that they were speaking about him. His misery grew. He gave up his search, crept slowly to the inner door and slid through it, wishing he might vanish away from the hospital, Brackenfield and England that very night and never see any of them again.

The consultant watched him go, glanced at his watch, sighed, said, "Always check everything, Frost. Remember most people are fools. Remember the higher you go the more fools you are responsible for."

"Yes, sir," said Colin. It was bitter, but it was true.

The consultant stared at the door through which Ahmed Patel had passed.

"How much longer do we have to endure that one?" he said.

CHAPTER THREE

Two days after the accident an inquest was held in Brackenfield upon the case of the dead man.

The coroner, working from papers before him and in the absence of a jury, passed over the question of identification at the start, calling instead upon the coach driver to give his account of the accident.

Among those waiting as witnesses, Colin Frost sat with Ahmed Patel and the staff nurse who had been in Casualty on the night in question. They had heard many times already the main facts of the collision. Patel was preoccupied by his abiding sense of guilt and by apprehension for his future, in spite of the fact that a solicitor from the medical insurance society to which he belonged was sitting at the table headed by the coroner and had spoken a few reassuring words to him before the beginning of the proceedings.

Colin Frost, still puzzled about the victim, but also bored by the coach driver's repetition, looked about him. He saw no one that seemed at all likely to be a relative of the deceased. On the other hand a second legal-looking character was sitting beside the one who was there to help Patty; acting for the family, without doubt, he decided.

The coach driver, wiping his sweaty forehead with a large clean handkerchief, which he next passed round inside his collar, climbed down from the witness box and resumed his seat at the far end of the row of witnesses. The senior officer of the police patrol took his place in the box, swore to speak the truth and waited. The coroner ran rapidly over the details of his name, profession and rank, after which the details of the accident began all over again.

Colin looked at his watch. They would be all day at it, at this rate. What was all this in aid of? Weren't they there to say what the chap died of? Did it matter how, when, where, or why the smash took place? The medical evidence. That was the coroner's pigeon. Or wasn't—

His attention came back to the witness box with a jerk.

"Yes, sir," the police officer was saying.

"You mean you were already searching for the car belonging to the deceased?"

"No, sir. The car the deceased was in did not belong to him. That was why I was looking for it, on information reported to Brackenfield police headquarters."

"Who did the car belong to?"

"A Mr Amos Gregson."

The coroner glanced at his papers.

"Yes," he said and paused, glancing at the line of witnesses as if to discover if Amos Gregson were among them. But almost at once he began again.

"I think you are telling me that you arrived on the scene very early, in the course of your search which ended there?"

"That is correct, sir. I radioed back to set up a diversion on the road and heard that a car had already telephoned from a call box near the town."

"That would be the car the coach driver asked to help him?"

"One of the passengers. Yes. The ambulance had already left when this call came through."

"How was that?"

"Another call had come in, reporting the accident and asking for an ambulance."

"A third call?" The coroner stared round the court. "This is very confusing. Please make clear to me the nature of these calls. And their order."

The patrol man sighed. He had foreseen the trouble. The coroner was elderly, conscientious, slow but sure.

"The woman's call was first, asking—"

"The woman? What woman?"

"She did not give her name and has not, so far, been traced."

"One of the coach passengers, I suppose?"

The coach driver rose to state in a loud voice that she blame well wasn't. He was subdued by a uniformed policeman and ignored by the coroner.

"Go on, officer," the latter urged.

"The woman asked for an ambulance. The passing car's owner asked for police and ambulance. I, having arrived meanwhile, asked for an ambulance and was told about the other two calls. The ambulance arrived very soon after."

With no sign of weariness the coroner took the patrol man through all those rescue operations in which he had taken part. Where this corresponded with the coach driver's account the coroner nodded his head. But he did not stop the flow and only very occasionally interrupted it.

At last the police witness stood down and the name of Amos Gregson was called. Whereupon a small stout man with a sagging face and red-rimmed eyes came out of the shadows at the back of the long room and moved reluctantly to the witness stand.

"You are Amos Gregson?"

"Yes."

"You run a—a recreation club—in Princes Street, Brackenfield?"

"That's right."

"The car involved in this accident, a Hillman, belonged to you?"

"That's my log book right under your nose. Number, registration, licence, the lot."

"There is no need to be impertinent. These things have to be verified. Did you lend your car to Mr Sparks?"

"I bloody well didn't! He pinched it and my best girl with it. Lucky for him—"

"Mr Gregson, if you can't keep a civil tongue in your head

and answer my questions quietly I shall have to charge
you with contempt of this court and let the law take its
course."

"He pinched it," Gregson repeated, suddenly subdued.
"He'd been making up to Clary ever since the first time he
came into the club."

"Who is Clary?"

"One of my girls. Hostess. Best looker, smart, too. Reliable, I
thought, till this happens."

The coroner looked round, helplessly.

"Did this young woman, Clary—"

"Clarice Field."

"Did Miss Field go away in your car with Mr Sparks without
your permission to leave her work?"

"Did she hell!"

"Where is she now? Why is she not here?"

"How should I know? Ask the rozzers. They should be interested."

Again the coroner looked round for help. This time he
caught the eye of Detective-Inspector Rawlinson, who nodded
very slightly. The coroner turned again to the club proprietor.

"You have seen the body? You identify it?"

"I've seen the body of a man I've known for the last five
weeks here in Brackenfield under the name of Jim Sparks. I
gave him a job in the bar of my club. I've been regretting it
ever since."

"You may stand down," said the coroner, "but do not leave
the court. I may need your assistance again."

Grumbling softly, Mr Gregson retreated to his former place
in the shadows and Inspector Rawlinson took the stand. After
the usual preliminaries the coroner shuffled his papers, then
looked up and said, "Your appearance in this case seems to be
due to somewhat unusual circumstances. Perhaps you would
indicate their nature to the court."

"Yes, sir. On the day of the accident we were notified in
Brackenfield from county headquarters that a certain indi-

vidual, who was believed to be residing here, was wanted for questioning. Full description of the person accompanied the request. I was detailed to deal with it and began my inquiries. I was informed of the road accident as soon as news of it came in. This led to my going to Brackenfield General Hospital, where I discovered, as I expected, that the seriously-ill casualty was the man I had been told to find."

"In other words you confirm that the man is the James or Jim Sparks described by the last witness?"

"No, sir."

"No?"

The coroner frowned at the sudden rustle and murmur from the body of the hall.

"Not exactly. The man was the one employed temporarily at Mr Gregson's club, but his real name was not Sparks."

"What was it, then?"

The inspector replied cautiously.

"The name given to us by county headquarters was Fred Holmes, but this is also thought to be an alias."

The Press, consisting of the two rival local papers and one freelance, began writing furiously. The freelance Colin recognised as the gaunt intruder in Casualty who had been thrown out so swiftly by the boss. This young man began to edge towards the end of the bench where all three journalists sat. Should he rush to phone now or wait for more? In an agony of suspense he waited and found a rich reward.

The coroner said, severely, "We are here to discover and record the cause of death of this man. We must, of course, record it in his true name, but I do not think we need to go fully into his past."

Here one of the two solicitors got to his feet and after a few exchanges with the coroner disclosed that to the best of his knowledge and belief the true name of Fred Holmes was Ivan Totteridge and he was born in 1920.

"Did you identify the body?"

"No. I never met the deceased. He was known personally to

the former senior members of my firm, all of whom have now retired or died."

"If the deceased has never seen you or consulted you, why are you here?"

"To represent the interest of a member of the family."

The coroner appealed to the police.

"Why was this member of the deceased's family not called to identify and give evidence?"

The answer was easy. The police had not been told of the existence of any member of the dead man's family.

"The matter cannot rest here," said the coroner, severely, turning again to the solicitor who had spoken. "But we will pass on now to the medical evidence."

The two St John ambulance men spoke in turn. Thomas Watts, the driver, explained how the injured man had recovered consciousness enough to direct him to the diary in his pocket.

"You say he recovered consciousness. To what do you ascribe his previous unconsciousness?"

"Concussion, shock and loss of blood," answered Watts, with confidence.

"Due solely to the accident?"

"Why yes, sir," answered Watts. "He relapsed into unconsciousness again almost at once."

The second man, Joe Gibson, described the journey to the hospital. He said he had loosened the tourniquet applied by the furniture van man, which had been on for more than fifteen minutes. A barely perceptible pulse did return at the wrist, but no bleeding recurred from the forearm, so he had left the tourniquet off. He had found the diary that Tom had told him of and discovered the page with the blood group written on it.

"You are familiar with the written description of a blood group?" asked the coroner.

"Yes, sir."

"Do you remember this one?"

Joe Gibson looked distressed.

"I'm afraid not. You see, I was very worried over the patient. He looked very bad. I was watching him and giving oxygen. I'd slipped the book in my pocket. I didn't register the group."

"But you went straight into the hospital to give the diary to the doctor on duty?"

"That is so."

And now the dread moment had arrived, Colin Frost thought; the moment he had waited for as the slow hours of the morning dragged along. He glanced at the Indian beside him. Patty had put on his best suit with a rather too exotic tie. His thick black hair shone with brilliantine, his dark face was shiny with sweat, his eyes were wide with fear.

"Good luck," whispered Colin. Patel's smile of thanks was more like a white grin of despair.

He was not in luck. To begin with, since he was a Hindu, he made an affirmation, which the coroner, being a practising Christian, privately considered less binding than the usual oath. Then the Indian's precise but not completely accurate English, spoken in a cultured voice, irritated the man who had never thought it necessary or desirable to modify his own flat Midlands accent. He listened, with growing prejudice, to the story of Patel's well-meaning but disastrous action. His questions, brief, searching, spoken in an acid voice that dissolved the remains of the Indian's morale, produced no real enlightenment for the coroner.

"How did you know that this blood group really was that of the injured man?"

"It was his diary. His name—"

"We have heard his real name was not Sparks."

"He had mentioned the blood group to the attendant of the ambulance."

"This blood group?"

Patel hung his head.

"I think perhaps not."

"I think that, too. Why did you not check by taking the patient's blood to the laboratory?"

"But I did so. I gave it to the technician for cross matching, but by the diary I took a bottle of the stated blood. I acted to save time. My intention was to save life."

"So I imagine. But you have, I see, medical qualifications. Do you not appreciate the value of the routine in the Casualty department? The routine that was followed with the specimen you took and subsequently disclosed your error? Your very grave error."

"It was to save time," Patel whispered, his throat dry with shame and fear.

"You did, however, take time to record from this diary the man's name and—"

"That I record very quickly. For necessary information. I copy also the blood group as I found in the little book. There you have proof that I speak truly."

"I have no proof. The book has not been found."

Again Ahmed Patel bowed his head. His grief and confusion had brought him very nearly to tears. He had nothing further to say in his own defence. He knew that this tiger of a coroner would accept no excuse, but was determined to prove him incompetent, dangerous, totally unworthy. He felt hot tears behind his eyelids blinding him as he groped his way back to his place among the witnesses.

Colin Frost, forthright and confident, described how he had met Patel coming from the laboratory with the blood; how he had set it up without question; how the patient had reacted; how he had later died.

"His multiple injuries were severe," he said. "This wrong blood may have helped to put him out, but there was enough there to kill him anyway."

Staff nurse told how she had followed the usual routine, helping Dr Patel to obtain blood and afterwards sending the student nurse on duty to the pathology department to fetch a second bottle which certainly would be needed. When Mr

Frost and Dr Patel arrived together, bringing blood, it did not occur to her that Dr Patel had not waited for the technician to match the blood he had taken from the patient.

"Were you not surprised this first bottle of blood was produced so quickly."

"I was far too concerned to get treatment started for this desperately ill man to bother with the time. We expect to get a drip going in ten minutes at the outside. Which we did."

This remark silenced the coroner for a couple of seconds, after which he dismissed the staff nurse and called the pathologist to give his account of the post-mortem.

"The man calling himself Jim Sparks appeared to be about forty-five years of age, five feet ten inches in height, weight—"

"We are trying to discover the cause of death," snapped the coroner. "You may omit the statistics. Give us an account of his injuries and whether or not you found any contributory disease."

"No contributory disease," said the pathologist, coldly. "Severe laceration of the right forearm and hand; a bruise, not severe, at the right side of the temporal bone, near the ear, no underlying fracture of the skull. A knife wound in the back on the left side, two inches in length and four inches deep, passing between the fourth and fifth ribs just to the outer edge of the scapula and penetrating the left lung in a downward direction. The haemorrhage from this wound and the arm injuries had been very severe. Taken with the shock of the accident, the total degree of shock was quite enough to cause death if unrelieved. Since the treatment given was more likely to intensify than relieve it, a fatal result was inevitable."

Ahmed Patel groaned aloud. Colin whispered to him to cheer up. The staff nurse glanced at the pathologist, who was an old enemy of hers. The coroner glanced at Inspector Rawlinson and summoned him once more to the witness stand.

"Why have we not been told before this that the victim of the accident was also the victim of a murderous assault?"

"The assault is still the subject of investigation," said the inspector, smoothly. "It was surmised from certain observations, made by the police patrol at the scene of the accident. It was located in the hospital shortly before death. Not by us."

The coroner was annoyed. Glaring at the Press he saw clearly that the criminal aspect of the case was likely to supercede even medical ineptitude. He recalled Patel, who now exhibited the boldness of despair.

"You examined the injured man on arrival, didn't you?"

"Yes, sir."

"You did not find this stab wound?"

"No, sir. I did not move the patient, who was lying on his back. I am glad I did not, as his weight applied the necessary pressure to the wound to prevent further haemorrhage."

"But did not prevent the lung from continuing to bleed inwardly," said the coroner. "Why did you not at once send for the surgical registrar to treat this very serious case?"

"He was sent for at once. I acted in his place till he arrived. He was asleep."

"Asleep? When on duty?"

"Mr Frost had been up all night, operating, on two nights before this. I myself one night. It is not possible to work all night and all day as well."

Colin confirmed that this was true. The second solicitor, who was watching the case on behalf of both him and Patel, now rose for the first time in their defence. Dr Patel, he said, was a junior houseman, qualified, but not experienced. He had taken the action, in good faith, that seemed to him to be the appropriate treatment for this case. No doctor could be blamed if his treatment, given in sincerity and to the best of his knowledge, was not successful. The errors arising over the treatment of this case were not unique. They were liable to happen in any hospital where inexperienced, or overworked staff were employed, where the establishment was under strength, where there were language difficulties, cultural differences of outlook, but above all, the solicitor insisted, where sweated labour was employed to deal with cases of life and death.

The Press scribbled madly, the coroner's face set hard. He agreed with every word the solicitor had spoken, but he felt no kinder towards Ahmed Patel. Also he disapproved of open propaganda in his court, however justified. On the other hand, Inspector Rawlinson had given him the cue he needed. The police were still investigating. He adjourned the inquest, but gave a certificate for burial.

Outside the court Ahmed Patel hurried away back to the hospital. He did not want to speak to anyone just then, not even to his friend, Colin Frost.

The latter went over to Inspector Rawlinson who was also about to move away on foot.

"I take it the chap was stabbed in the car?" he said. "So someone was there with him? Apart from the girl, I mean. We didn't have her in as a casualty, by the way."

"He could hardly have been stabbed outside the car," answered the inspector mildly. "But the girl might have done it."

"I suppose so. Before the accident, or after? I mean, did it *cause* the accident?"

"Possibly. I think not likely. The assailant does not appear to have been suicidal. Quite the opposite."

"Have you got him? Or her? Do you really know who did it?"

"Not yet."

Colin frowned.

"My point is that the lung injury was going to be fatal anyway. Patty's boob didn't really make so much difference. We got some of the right stuff in before it was too late."

"But he died. You *were* too late."

"What I mean is, when you produce evidence of murder or manslaughter, that'll have to be the verdict, won't it? And let Patty out."

"Look," said the inspector, beginning to move away. "I respect your loyalty to your profession, but this character, Sparks or Holmes or Totteridge or whatever, was an old lag and a very constant bloody nuisance to every police force in the country. Now he's gone where his conning no longer bothers us and we're grateful. Misadventure would save us a wonderful lot of trouble."

"It might ruin a doctor who hopes to do a lot of good in his own country when he's ready for it."

"Our profession is overworked and underpaid, too, doctor," said Rawlinson, with feeling.

For a few seconds Colin watched the straight back moving up the street. Then he turned to walk away in the opposite direction.

CHAPTER FOUR

In the residents' common room at Brackenfield General that night the case was discussed with great freedom and some ribaldry. But through it all ran a thread of loyalty, first to their profession, that had been lowered by an indefensible mistake, secondly to the hospital struggling against growing odds to provide a reasonable service to the genuinely sick and injured, and last but by no means the least felt, a wave of protective loyalty to poor little Patty, so eager, so willing, so obliging in the matter of standing in for night work and weekends. Given his nationality, his far from British outlook and his unprofessional impulsiveness, he had acted entirely in character. It was unfair that this latest exploit had brought about disaster.

"I still say the chap was on the way out, regardless," Colin repeated for perhaps the hundredth time.

"The coroner'll never wear it," he was told. "You said yourself the police couldn't care less who stuck a knife into him. They've wanted him dead for years, you said."

"Then I don't see them putting J. Sparks on their priority list for the full treatment," another voice agreed.

The medical registrar, looking round the room, said, "Where's Patty now? He was in at dinner."

A cynical voice suggested, "Mulling over the most comfortable way of committing suicide, I expect."

"Probably. He's a great lad for the textbooks."

Colin got up and left them to it. They meant no harm—they all liked Patty; who wouldn't? But they had no opinion of his basic ability, his fundamental grasp of the essentials of disease, the basic requirements of treatment. Colin believed, on the contrary, that the Indian had them, that his main difficulty was Western technical brilliance, the immense detail of the new mechanical and chemical treatments, the importance of organising accurately every step in this forest of detail where Patty had lost his way.

He arrived at the Indian's door and knocked. A calm voice asked him to go in. Patel was sitting very close to a small electric fire whose bluish-red, faint glow proclaimed the usual evening power cut. Patel was reading a modern treatise on haematology. The page was open at a section on blood groups. His face was rigid with concentration, but not any longer, Colin was relieved to see, with despair.

"Sorry to interrupt," he said. "I'll go if you'd rather."

"No," said Patel, getting up to give his visitor the armchair he had been sitting in and to draw forward the only other chair in the tiny room. "No. I have found where I was wrong."

"Have you? You mean why the blood you got was incompatible?"

"That, too. My fault was as usual. A crisis. I excite. I take—I snatch—an idea. I run. It is the wrong idea."

"Hardly an idea. You took a written down statement. That's what I came to see you about. Have you found that diary yet?"

"No. I have been twice more to look. I find nothing. The nurses are not pleased."

"I don't imagine they'd pinch it themselves. But I wouldn't put it past the cleaners."

"To sweep it up, you mean? Then it goes to the incinerator. It is lost."

"Perhaps not. A little diary, thrown away. It would appeal to Mrs Obefema. Isn't that her name? Head cleaner in out-patients. Very black, very stout, always laughing."

Patel winced.

"I could not ask her. She is from East Africa. They do not like my race. Always when I pass her she laughs behind my back. It disturbs me. Many years ago these people were our slaves. Now they hate us and despise."

"Don't worry. They've got *us* down as slave-drivers in chief. I always thought it was the Arabs who ran the real slave trade on the spot and we did our best to upset it."

"Before you went to East Africa we bought from the Arabs."

"O.K. If you don't feel up to tackling her, I will. She's quite a friend of mine since I sewed up one of her brats that had cut himself on a piece of glass he was trying to use on another kid."

The next morning Colin went early to out-patients and found Mrs Obefema. His interesting story, his earnest manner, his hints of police investigation produced results. Mrs Obefema said she thought the book had turned up in one of the wastepaper baskets that very morning. She would rescue it if possible from the incinerator and put it in his pigeon hole beside the staff letter board in the main hall.

A few hours later the diary was there, intact except for a few pages rather raggedly torn out from the middle. Colin showed it to Patel, who took it gingerly, leafed through it reluctantly and handed it back.

"She took it herself," he said, with disgust. "It has her smell."

"Now then," said Colin, who had reached both these conclusions "no racial discrimination. You'd swear to the book, I suppose?"

"Oh, yes. And the blood group is there, the one I fetched.

Only now I see it is possible the letter has been changed."

"*What!*"

"This is what I saw. I copied on the patient's notes. I fetched—"

"Oh, my God!"

Colin was aghast. Looking carefully he saw that the group written, B.Rh+ could have been altered from A.Rh+ if the A had been written with upright sides and a rounded top. To convert it to B would need only a line across the bottom. The lines of the letter did appear to be all of the same colour, the same thickness. But, as Patty said, it was possible the base line had been added.

This made matters worse than ever. Before the diary was found he had concluded that some enemy of the man Sparks had written in the wrong group, which Patel had copied in good faith. Would an altered writing carry the same conclusion? Or would the coroner, already prejudiced, decide that the alterer could very well be Patel himself, bent on producing evidence in his own favour? That the entry had been altered was now almost certain. Not put down wrong deliberately, but deliberately changed to bring about, at whatever time it was used, a lethal rather than a healing result.

So the vital question was, when? Had Sparks been recognised at the scene of the accident, before the ambulance bore him away? Very few people had been in contact with him then, he understood from the inspector's evidence, though one had given proof of murderous intent. However, the hand that thrust the knife into Sparks's back was unlikely to have been the same that altered a piece of writing, carefully, neatly, so that only close attention, possibly expert tests, could reveal it.

The change in the diary must have been made before the accident, Colin decided. How long before and by whom? He searched the little book closely, cursing himself for his slow wits.

Sparks had written very little; most of the pages were blank.

The others held only groups of figures with nothing to suggest what they referred to. Patty, who had flipped through the book when first he held it, was sure none was missing at that time.

"Mrs Obefema tore them out," he said. It certainly looked like it, Colin decided. But the fact that finally roused Colin's impatience with himself was plain on the faded, roughened surface of the corner of the diary. The date, 1957.

Jim Sparks had kept this obsolete diary, probably carrying it with him always. It held a piece of information he would not ever wish to be without. His blood group.

Why? Some previous accident or illness, where the knowledge had been needed for his recovery? During all these years the diary had been seen and its value understood by how many others? Friends and enemies? How many? Which of them had altered the precious statement and was perhaps even now reading the newspaper account of the pathologist's evidence with satisfaction at the success of a well-planned, subtle, undetectable revenge?

Colin made up his mind to find out. He was due for a fortnight's leave from the coming Friday evening. He had arranged to go to his parents' home, but they would not mind if he changed his plans. He had already decided to find out more about Jim Sparks. Not from the police. Inspector Rawlinson had shown clearly that he was not interested. Besides, Sparks had never lived in Brackenfield until he took the job at Gregson's club. His past lay elsewhere. The man to disclose it was the solicitor who had spoken at the inquest and who, presumably, would be making the arrangements for the disposal of the corpse.

Colin, after spending a short time with Patel, explaining the significance of the date of the diary, went to the hospital mortuary. Here he learned what he wanted to know. A Mr Dodds had called at the hospital directly after the inquest was adjourned, bringing with him Brackenfield's best-known undertaker. Together with the mortuary attendant, the two men

had arranged for Sparks to be sent to the village of Twitbury
St Mary, in Berkshire, where he would be buried. Mr Dodds
had left his own address. He had not mentioned the proposed
date of the funeral, but he had asked that the place of it be
withheld from the Press.

"Very anxious to avoid publicity," the attendant said.
"Which is natural, seeing what sort the deceased appears to
have been."

"I won't tell them," Colin promised. "But I think I'll have a
look at Twitbury St Mary."

After careful thought he decided not to write to the
solicitor. He knew he would get no useful information from
him about the family of the dead man. His time from mid-
night on Friday was his own for two weeks. He might just as
well explore Twitbury St Mary as any other part of the country
hitherto unvisited.

He also decided not to take Patty to the funeral, though the
Indian, still guilt-ridden, still contrite, wanted to meet a relative to whom he could express his sorrow. But he accepted
Colin's judgment in the matter. The fact that all his junior
colleagues at the hospital were on his side comforted him
greatly. He even felt a little embarrassed by Colin's
enthusiasm.

"You should not do so much on my behalf," he protested.
"You are my friend but I have played the fool, isn't it? And do
not deserve you may risk—"

"I'm not risking anything," Colin reassured him. "What I
choose to do with my leave is entirely my own affair. Actually,
you are the only person who knows where I'm going and why."

Twitbury St Mary was a moderate-sized village with an
ancient centre set about its twelfth-century church and several
much later extensions built along the three roads leading from
it. One of these was clearly late Victorian and Edwardian; large,
gabled houses with generous drives and ample gardens, built
no doubt for retired service men and their families or for early
commuters on the developing railways to Reading, Oxford or

London. Twitbury station, now derelict, had served not only Twitbury St Mary, but Twitbury All Souls and Netherbury, a hamlet that had faded almost completely until the Second World War, when a factory for making parachutes, transferred from a heavily bombed area, came to rest there and prospered. The new council estate at Twitbury St Mary now merged with Netherbury council houses to cover all the land that had in former times provided a living in farming for the village clustered about the ancient church.

Colin came into Twitbury from Netherbury, growing more and more depressed by the endless rows of redbrick boxes and their neat council-mown grass verges. He had expected an old-world, picturesque setting. He had already decided that some romantic tragedy must have led to Jim Sparks's sordid end. Netherbury was about as romantic as a self-help multiple food store, two of which he had seen as he came through the area.

However, the church was rewarding to look at, and the small old pub opposite, though not able to offer him a bed, recommended a hiker's hostel a few doors away. The warden of this establishment, though astonished to find anyone travelling on holiday in late October, even in a car, was willing to provide a reasonably furnished cubicle with a modern mattress on the bed and a wash-hand basin where the hot tap provided scalding water.

In addition to these amenities the warden was able to give valuable information. He knew that a grave was being dug in the churchyard that very day, or rather an existing grave was being opened. A funeral was due to take place the next morning.

"A well-known local family, I suppose?" Colin asked, trying to conceal his excitement.

"In a manner of speaking," the warden answered. "But there don't be above half a dozen old folk who knew the last one living here. Moved away, I'm told, after the last war. I didn't come here myself till after they'd gone. But Tom Benson knows. Him that's seeing to the grave and that."

Colin thanked him and wandered out, to take a look round the village, he told the warden. But once out of sight of the hostel's front windows he hurried to the churchyard, where he found an elderly man at work, whom he took to be Tom Benson.

Guessing rightly that the old fellow would stay at work until noon, Colin went first into the church. There was not much of interest to see there, the usual modest furnishings, two vases of late chrysanthemums on the altar, a few brasses and stone tablets to the dead decorating the walls. He went out again quite soon and began to study the tombstones and other monuments in the churchyard, working his way unostentatiously to where Tom Benson was digging.

"There seems to be a number of this name here," he said, thoughtfully, pausing beside the man.

"Stowdens? Aye, they come 'ere in my granfer's time. That was the old colonel, James Stowden, retired after the Boer War, when 'e come 'ere with 'is family. Lost the eldest son, another James, in the First World War. You'll 'ave seen mention of 'im inside."

He waved his hand towards the church and Colin nodded.

"There was two younger sons, though, come through it. One of 'em married and took the house 'ere after the old man died. 'E had one son, James again and a couple of girls. The boy went in the Army too. Fine-looking young chap. They was both in it, the Second War. Father killed, young James not. Mother and sisters worked in London and died in the blitz."

"That would be the other memorial in the church? The long one, to Roger Stowden and his wife and daughters? I forget their names."

"That's right. His body was brought home to this grave. Theirs wasn't never found. None of 'em."

"The family was wiped out, then?"

"Except for young James and 'is uncle, William. Brigadier Stowden, that is. Bachelor all his life. Lives hereabouts, not in the old house. They never come back to that."

"Then who—?"

Colin pointed at the prepared grave where Tom Benson was now placing planks in readiness for the committal.

"Captain James. At least, 'e left the army after the war. 'Ad enough soldiering, I reckon. Mr James, I suppose I should say."

He turned away, a gesture that Colin took to be a form of dismissal. However, he walked off with increased knowledge and a firm conviction that the man who had called himself Jim Sparks, Fred Holmes and Ivan Totteridge was in fact a Stowden, perhaps the last of the branch that had settled in Twitbury St Mary.

The dead man's family history was not unusual. A standard army background, the tradition passing down from father to son. A veteran of the African wars, retiring to the country in the early years of the century; then First World War tragedy, the heir killed, two younger sons surviving. A Second World War holocaust, only the black sheep left. And the brigadier.

James Stowden to Jim Sparks. Colin walked away, thinking over what he had been told. He had the beginning, the origins. There was most of a lifetime to fill. Though he visited the pub again that evening and tried once or twice to lead the conversation to local events he failed to hear any more of the Stowden family. Probably, as the warden had said, there were very few people left in the village who had known the Stowdens when they lived there. It was not as if they were a long established, or noble or historical family. Not even one of the former gentry, whose elderly unmarried women still lingered in converted cottages. The Stowdens had barely ceased to be foreigners when war had gobbled them up. Except for James, unlucky, orphaned, criminal James.

And of course the uncle, Colin reminded himself the next day in the churchyard, standing respectfully with a handful of spectators while the coffin was lowered into the grave where the older Stowden lay at a deeper level. The uncle. That other fighting son of the Boer War veteran, who had undoubtedly survived the Second World War and distinguished himself in his career and now stood, a tubby but erect white-haired figure on the righthand side of the clergyman, with the solicitor, Robin Dodds on the right again.

Colin recognised Dodds. The solicitor, glancing up with suddenly enlightened eyes, recognised Colin. The young man was aware of this, but made no sign. Dodds, on the other hand, as soon as the ceremony was over, began to speak rapidly to the old man at his side. But before the two could move away, Colin had come up to them, blocking the narrow path between the graves.

"General Stowden?" he began.

"Brigadier," said Dodds, sourly.

"I beg your pardon, sir. Brigadier Stowden?"

"Well?" the latter said, looking from his solicitor to the intelligent, embarrassed face of the newcomer.

"I was in charge of—of your late nephew's case, sir," Colin said. "In Casualty, I mean, after the accident."

"Well?" said the brigadier again. He found his thoughts wandering back down the years, filled with countless young, intelligent, embarrassed junior officers trying to explain away their frequent errors. "Well?" he repeated mildly.

To his surprise Colin found himself encouraged, not intimidated. He gave a rapid, non-technical account of what had gone wrong. Also of what had been said at the inquest and the danger to Patel's career.

Brigadier Stowden turned to Dodds.

"I thought Jim died of his injuries in the car crash," he said. "Why have you kept these complications from me, Robin?"

"I thought—I thought—"

"You thought the less the old dodderer knew the better, I suppose?"

"Not really. I know how much—"

"What's your name, Doctor?"

"Colin Frost, sir."

"Well, Dr Frost, I want to hear what you know in more detail and not standing here catching pneumonia. So the least I can do is offer you luncheon and take you home with me."

"I'm staying in the village until tomorrow," Colin said. "But thank you very much, if I can get a bus back afterwards."

"Mr Dodds will bring you back afterwards," said the brigadier. "Won't you, Robin? It'll be on your own way home."

"Of course," said Dodds, without enthusiasm.

After an excellent plain lunch Colin felt even more encouraged than before. Having gone over all the detail of Jim Sparks's unfortunate death, he described how Patel had made his fatal mistake, how the diary had disappeared, how it had now been recovered.

"You see it was so natural of Patty—Dr Ahmed Patel—to act as he did. He's such a good chap, really. He'll be splendid back home in more primitive—no, I don't mean that—less exacting conditions, technically. I don't expect you know Indians, sir, but—"

"*Not know Indians!*" the brigadier exploded. "I spent twelve years of my service in India between the wars. I know exactly what you mean about this Dr—Patel, did you say? Hindu, of course. Brahmin?"

"I—I'm afraid I don't know."

"No. Why should you?"

Colin was silent. It was the first time the not-so-distant past had rushed up to him demanding attention. Between the wars. The British Empire. Kipling. No, Kipling was earlier. Or was he? He felt confused and ignorant, but the old boy was speaking again, so he forced himself to listen.

"You didn't come here simply to give me the details of my nephew's death. Perhaps you were afraid I might try to take action against you and your assistants for negligence. I assure you it's the last thing I'd do. The poor fellow is at peace now."

Seeing Colin's face change he added, "You know something more about him, don't you?"

"Only what was said at the inquest."

"More deception, Robin?"

"I didn't want to distress you."

"But you knew I read the papers. I agree the name ... But there have been so many—"

"I don't understand," Colin said, gently, when the pause seemed to lead nowhere. "Your nephew was in the army under his own name, I believe?"

"He was. At the end of the war he was Captain James Stowden, recommended for a gong he never received."

"Why not, sir?"

"Because he was cashiered, Dr Frost. Dismissed with ignominy. He never used his own name again."

CHAPTER FIVE

Detective-Inspector Rawlinson was not getting on very well. His superintendent, impressed by the full detail of the adjourned inquest, realised that they must make a greater effort to find the person who had stabbed the dead man. On the showing of the patrol man's evidence a woman had been in the car on the evening of the accident, though there was nothing except the telephone call to confirm that she had been there at the time it happened. Surely she had not been suicidal to the point of pushing a knife between the ribs of the man who was driving her? If not, then had she done so after the accident? Directly after the accident, it must have been. Then, leaving the car before the coach driver or anyone else had been capable of seeing her, had she first thrown the knife down near the ditch and then run away towards the telephone a quarter of a mile further back on the Brackenfield road? All most improbable. A third person, then? In the car? A hidden assassin or an accomplice of the woman, or a jealous friend of hers? People do not hide easily in cars in real life. They make big shadows, they make small noises, they smell of their tobacco, their drink, their hair oil, their soap or the lack of it. All the same, a second man, an attacker, could not be lightly discarded.

Inspector Rawlinson sighed. It all boiled down to finding the woman. Clarice Field. Ex-hostess at the local dance club and vice dive. Amos Gregson's favourite among his brassy hostesses. She, too, had been identified. She always used her real name, Clarice Field. She had been associated with Sparks when he was Fred Holmes. She had been put away for six months for harbouring him when he got two years for false pretences, just one year and four months ago. She was loyal. She had kept in touch after her own release and had got him his last job, here in Brackenfield. She had now disappeared.

The police had wasted no time on the night of the accident. Gregson's complaint about his car and his hostess had been made before the car crashed. Though Sparks lived at the club, Miss Field had kept her old lodgings in the town. It had taken her no time at all on release, to find her job with Amos Gregson. It might have been made for her. Inspector Rawlinson was not at all sure it hadn't. But now she had disappeared.

Grumbling very much, but aware that the stab wound had ruined their chances of getting an uncluttered inquest verdict of misadventure, Rawlinson and the superintendent agreed that the woman would have to be found and when found induced to tell all she knew about the supposed third traveller in the car. To find her they would need to question everyone on the staff of the club and also get co-operation from London, where Field and Sparks had lived until the con man's activities had again gone beyond fines, admonishing, probation and on one occasion corrective training, against which he had successfully appealed.

There were five other girls employed at Gregson's club, two in the bar, one in the so-called powder room and the remaining two as hostesses on the dance floor. Clarice Field had made a third with these two.

"Clary was worth the pair of them put together," Gregson

D

repeated, when the inspector asked to speak to the girls.

"Where did you get her from, exactly?"

"Joint in Chelsea. She'd been away for a while, as you no doubt know. The manager wanted to take her on again but the other girls cut up rough. He knew me. So he recommended her."

"And you took her on? Bit of a risk, wasn't it?"

"I didn't see it that way. She said she wanted to make a fresh start. After all, she was only in for harbouring, wasn't she? Well, they all say that about a fresh start. But with her looks and training—she's a first-rate dancer and that went in her favour. The other two have looks, but no personality, if you see what I mean, and dance no more idea than a—"

"I'd like to have a word with them, all the same," Rawlinson interrupted. "Separately, if you don't mind."

"You can use my office," Gregson said.

The first girl had nothing of interest to tell the inspector. She had disliked Clarice Field, was jealous of her and took no trouble to hide it. Rawlinson cut short her spiteful, scurrilous conclusions and quite blatant hindsight. He asked her to send along her colleague, Ivy.

"I don't know where she is, you'd better ask Mr Amos," she said, opening the door with a jerk that revealed Ivy still in a crouching position at the level of the keyhole.

"Come in," said Rawlinson, smoothly.

Ivy was confused; upset by her exposure. She expected an attack, a reprimand. When instead she was offered a chair she collapsed on to it and began to cry. After that, which again provoked no anger or blame, she was ready to help the inspector even to the extent of speaking the truth.

"Oh yes," she said, having established that friendship of a sort had existed between her and the missing Clarice. "Oh yes, we went about a lot when she first came. Not so much after she began going out with this fellow."

"Jim Sparks?"

"*No!*" This was spoken in a voice of great scorn. "No, he

never came to the club. This boy-friend, I mean. It was one
night we was going to see a picture she was keen on. Not me,
not my type."

"The actor in the film or this man?"—

"The film, of course. We saw it and directly we left Clary
pointed across the road and said, 'See that guy with the funny
little hat, over there?' and I said, 'Yah. You know him?' And
she said, 'You betcher! I'll have to speak to him. Don't wait.'
So she crossed the road to him. Mind you, he never looked our
way. Never moved an eyelash, not even when she got to him.
Just turned and walked off and she nearly running on her
stilettoes to keep up."

"Did she ever tell you who he was? His name, job, address?"

"Never. Always called him 'my chap', never no name."

"But she did go out with him a lot?"

"I wouldn't know. She never went out with me again. Not
after that night. Nice as pie here in the club. But I never saw
her again outside it."

"Did this go on after Jim Sparks began to work in the bar
here?"

"How do I know? She knew Jim all right and we knew she
did, because it was her got him the job. We thought he was
her brother or a relation of some sort."

"Could she have been his wife?"

Ivy burst into loud laughter.

"Clary couldn't be anyone's wife. Not for more than a
couple of hours, she couldn't."

Inspector Rawlinson left the club, cursing the meagreness of
the information he had gathered there. Clarice Field, convicted
of harbouring a criminal, had seemingly taken up with another
of her acquaintance while Sparks, as Fred Holmes, was still
serving his sentence. Who was this likely to be, what had he
been doing on the night of the accident, was he still in Brackenfield?

Gregson, anxious to get rid of the inspector before the club
opened for the evening, could not or would not provide

answers to these questions. Clary had never hidden the fact
that she was an old friend of Jim's. He, Gregson, would not
have taken the man on otherwise. He knew he'd been in
trouble, too. Clary had turned out well, so why shouldn't Jim?

Rawlinson listened to this simple drivel, as he considered it,
with a sardonic smile. Gregson refused to be provoked. The
inspector went away to Miss Field's former lodgings to make
another attempt to establish the second man. But he did not
succeed. Jim Sparks had sometimes called for Miss Field,
sometimes had arrived in her company, often brought her
home at night. No other man had ever done any of these
things.

So the next move had to be made in London. Here co-
operation opened a few windows on an extended view of Miss
Field's career, but at the same time increased Inspector
Rawlinson's work. Jim Sparks had been convicted five years
before his second major offence and had been sentenced to
three years for fraud. At that time, seven years ago, he was
calling himself Ivan Totteridge. Also at that time he had a
wife.

"Not the woman calling herself Clarice Field?"

"Certainly not. We lost track of Mrs Totteridge after he was
put inside. No reason for keeping up. I think I'm right in
saying she had already cut loose and never visited him."

"Did Field? I mean was she in the picture then?"

"Far too young, I should think. You could ask at the nick."

"Was he in the same one both times?"

"Yes, he was. And Field was certainly the girl-friend the
second time he went down. At least, she visited regularly, after
she'd come out herself. The question was did she do it for
personal reasons or professionally?"

"I don't quite get. I thought—"

"I know what you thought and you're right. Nothing doing.
But Field has been for years on the fringe of a very shifty set
of villains. Shifty and shifting."

"How's that?"

"Set of specialists. No master mind. Never is, properly speaking. They work on a sort of register. Get together exactly the team they want for a job. Holmes—he was Holmes when we began to notice him again, acted for them in casing their projects. We could never prove a thing against him."

"Then why—?"

"He didn't only work for the group, or team or whatever. He ran his own line outside it. Made the mistake of his life."

"I thought that came five years earlier?"

"Well, yes, perhaps it did."

"So Clarice Field belonged to the group and this other man, the one I'm after, might be one of them?"

"Might very well be one of them. Seems to have been living in Brackenfield lately, does he?"

Inspector Rawlinson was mortified by his complete ignorance on this point, but he had to acknowledge it. The Yard man merely nodded.

"Fair enough. He could easily commute from Brackenfield, probably in someone else's car. They economise in travel, these lads. I'll work the grapevine and let you know."

"The point is," said Rawlinson, trying to prove his own competence, "we have evidence there was a woman in the car with Sparks and the knife handle shows several blotched prints, probably hers. We don't think it's likely she stabbed Sparks herself, either before the accident, risking her own neck, or after, because she must have left the car immediately to get back along the road to the phone box as fast as she did. She could have taken the knife though and thrown it down on the grass, aiming at the ditch."

"Or there might, as you said, have been a third person in the car, member of this gang I've mentioned, jealous of Sparks, furious at the accident ruining whatever it was they were up to, stuck him in a fit of temper, or jitters or plain jealousy?"

"After or before the crash?"

"Before would certainly cause it. After more likely, I'd say. I'll let you know if anything crops up."

So Rawlinson went back to Brackenfield where he found a
pile of routine work waiting for him. He spent a couple of days
straightening this out, while hoping for a message from London that did not come. On the third day, however, two pieces
of information arrived within an hour or two of each other. If
they had not been so close he might never have put them
together. As it was, his instant hunch proved rewarding.

The first was a telephone call from a lodging house keeper
on the outskirts of the town. This was a respectable widow
who provided bed and breakfast for up to four workers on
building sites around the town. The men came and went, being
the type of casual labourer, near tramp, who never settled in
any one place, but was continually moving away after the
rough work on any particular site was finished.

The woman rang up to say a man who had lodged with her
for the last three weeks had left his car outside her door one
night, had not slept in his bed, but had taken his belongings
and disappeared. The car was still there. The children weren't
doing it any good. Didn't the police think they ought to take it
away?

The second message came from an irate farmer, five miles
outside Brackenfield, complaining that a man had tramped
straight across two fields of winter crops, broken the padlock
on one gate and the wire on another, leaving both wide open
so that two horses in the next field had gone in and increased
the devastation.

Both these incidents had taken place on the night of the
Hillman accident. The delay in their coming to Rawlinson's
notice would normally have blown up a first-class row at the
station, but since they had given him an idea he passed this
over, for the time being at any rate.

A detective-sergeant was sent at once to look at the aban-
doned car, discover if the widow was owed any money and get
a full description of the man who had left her room without
notice. He himself went to see the farmer.

The latter was delighted to have such prompt, even eager

attention from the police. It was not the first time his farm
had suffered from hooligans but on previous occasions he had
not met with any success or official help in tracing the culprits.

This time it was very different. The inspector wanted to
follow the exact course the marauder had taken. He walked
with the farmer across the two damaged fields along a track of
footprints very well marked, coming away from the road and
which led to the exact spot on it where the crash had taken
place. The inspector went up and down inside the hedge beside
the road. He found one place where the twigs were bent aside,
some broken. Below this point the ground was trampled hard.

The farmer watched and understood.

"Came away from the road, or got out on it?" he asked.
"Making a short cut over my land whichever way it was."

"That's right," said Rawlinson. He marked one footprint,
just inside the hedge, clearer than the rest, for further treatment. Then he and the farmer went back the way they had
come.

The footprint might be helpful, Rawlinson thought. He
proposed to search the broken gate and its padlock for finger-
prints, but did not expect to find any. There had been none
identified in the car except those of Jim Sparks and Clarice
Field. The rest, not matched in police records, probably belonged to the various helpers at the time of the accident.
There was no proof, so far, that the man who had hidden
behind the hedge, who had tramped across the fields, stupidly
and provocatively forcing the two gates, was the owner and
wielder of the knife found near the ditch. No proof that he
was the same who had lodged at the widow's house, who had
left a small, old, much-used car outside it when he went away
without notice. But it was material to work on at last and
Inspector Rawlinson was encouraged to go forward with
renewed energy.

He was rewarded—to a limited extent. In due course tests
were made, results correlated and checked. The little old car
had been stolen in London six weeks ago. It had been sprayed

black over its original grey. It had false number plates. The man who had lodged with the widow and worked on a demolition site was a member of the group of 'specialists'. He had a record of five convictions. He had been in the same prison as Sparks during the first of the latter's sentences. He had at one time been living with Clarice Field. His name, or the one he had used for the last ten years, was Alec Hilton.

The main clues leading to this identification had been found in the room the man had left so hurriedly. But Rawlinson's footprint also confirmed his presence on the farmer's land.

So far so good. But where did it lead? Back to Miss Field, the inspector decided, with a feeling of helplessness. And the woman who could complete the story, who knew exactly what had happened in that Hillman, on that road, on that dark misty October evening, was not to be found. Not in Brackenfield, not at any of her usual haunts in London or her usual lodgings there. The informer grapevine could not, or more probably would not, given an answer of any kind. Clarice had well and truly gone to ground.

This was natural, Inspector Rawlinson decided, all things considered. She knew far too much, in many directions. She had apparently been going off with Sparks, or at any rate been engaged with him upon some project of his own that involved the suicidally rash theft of Gregson's car. A sudden impulse? Unplanned? Certainly an act on the woman's part that put her in the worst possible light with the other 'specialists'. Hilton had made no preparations to leave Brackenfield in a hurry. He had gone without taking the simplest precautions.

Inspector Rawlinson sighed. The girl was right to disappear. The lack of news on the grapevine supported this view. The future would show, or might never show, whether her disappearance had been her own doing or brought about by those associates she had not been able to discard.

Inspector Rawlinson sighed again. That coroner's verdict of misadventure, of accidental injuries accelerated to a fatal conclusion by a foreign doctor's competence, receded into the distance. Nothing could now alter the importance of the stab wound and the possibility that it had been the direct cause of collision with the coach and therefore of the death of Sparks. Nothing. Not even the testimony of Field, who was still missing. In any case the adjournment of the inquest must stand. Indefinitely.

Inspector Rawlinson turned with reluctance, with a sense of exasperation, to those other tasks, routine and mundane, that had continued to multiply on his desk during so many disappointing days.

CHAPTER SIX

Colin arrived back at the hostel from the brigadier's house in mid-afternoon. The solicitor had been rather more friendly during the drive to Twitbury St Mary. This was partly because the old man had not seemed to suffer too much from discussing his late troublesome nephew and partly because he wanted to clear up, as far as the young man could help him, the real cause of the unfortunate man's death.

Colin was quite ready to explain further Patel's action, which still seemed to him hardly blameable at all.

"He wasn't to know his information from the chap's diary was wrong," he repeated once more. "I know he should have waited for the blood to be cross-matched. He knew the routine, but he hadn't really grasped the full technical meaning of it. He hasn't got that kind of mind. They don't have; not the ordinary run of them."

"Asiatics, or all coloured citizens?" Dodds asked.

"The qualified doctors are nearly all Indian or Pakistani. It isn't that they don't know their stuff. They do. They know the textbooks backwards. This was something he had to *do*. The actual apparatus for applying the principles. Patty doesn't *think* in terms of mechanics or mechanisms. When he goes home he won't have to. Not so much. Not for a long time. They haven't got it all laid on everywhere by any means. Not yet."

"You are very keen on his defence."

"Of course I am. He's a personal friend of mine."

Mr Dodds thought this over. The young man's attitude was praiseworthy, he considered. He had no racial prejudice himself, he believed, but he knew his attitude had never been tested. He did know, however, being a man of honest and analytical mind, that he had not felt in the least sympathetic towards the witness when Patel had given his evidence in the coroner's court.

"Anyway," Colin said, as Dodds remained silent, "now we have found the diary we know the entry in it is a lie, a deliberate lie. A vital change was made. I don't know when or by whom, but I'm going to find out if I can."

"Take it to the police, you mean?"

"Not unless I have to. It depends what happens. I mean, if they find the one who stuck the knife in the poor chap. Also what the coroner decides at the inquest when it comes on again. If it's murder by stabbing, or by causing a car smash by stabbing, bringing about multiple injuries, with no mention of Patty's boob, I'll keep it to myself. But I'd still very much like to know."

"I shouldn't think you ever will," said Dodds. But he spoke kindly, even regretfully, as if sad to find no answering spark in himself to match his young companion's eagerness.

Colin went to his room at the hostel with far less assurance than he had tried to display to the solicitor. But he decided to go for a walk to get rid of a certain drowsiness he felt and that he put down to an unexpectedly ample lunch with wine at the meal and brandy to follow. Arranged, as he was well aware, not for his entertainment but for Mr Dodds's benefit and to cheer up the old soldier himself. It was not until the evening that Colin began to understand that his drowsiness and general lethargy might also be due to an accumulation of fatigue from chronic overwork, too few hours of sleep and too much nagging responsibility. He decided to spend another day at Twitbury St Mary. After all, he was committed to research into James Stowden's past. There must be some of the locals who remembered him.

But here he was disappointed. Brigadier Stowden had retired to his present house near Twitbury in the middle fifties. His nephew had come there at very infrequent intervals and had never stayed for more than a day or two. He had been known at the house and in the village as Mr James, the newer inhabitants not quite understanding if this was his first or his surname and no one much interested to find out. There had been one occasion, according to a local farmer Colin met in the pub, who was willing to discuss the family with him, an occasion when the nephew had borrowed money—the farmer did not say from whom—and left without paying it back. The brigadier had paid and that was the end of it. There was no point in digging up old scandals, the farmer said. They all liked the old man and respected him. He had mentioned this story as a warning that the past was not all it should have been.

Colin took it as a warning that the past, being dead and now buried locally, should not be dug up again and that Twitbury St Mary had no intention of aiding his excavations.

Perhaps the warden at his hostel knew more. But the man had referred him to Tom Benson, the gravedigger. Tom, then? He had come up with the early history readily enough, but had shut up at once when it came to Mr James. All things considered, Colin decided to leave the next morning.

However, a note arrived for him in the middle of the afternoon from Brigadier Stowden, asking him to call at his convenience and preferably that evening about nine. No reason was given for this invitation, but the summons filled Colin with hope. He had no doubt he would learn more about the early years of James Stowden, alias Jim Sparks, than the cautious neighbours had been willing to tell him.

He was right. Brigadier Stowden greeted him in a calm

friendly manner, offered him drink and tobacco, which latter he refused and settled him in a comfortable chair before a cheerful log fire.

"I told you too much and not enough yesterday," the old man began. "I don't want you stirring up the district to get the rest of the story. Not that they're very forthcoming, here-abouts."

"They aren't," said Colin.

The other nodded.

"Exactly. Thinking it over, I feel I owe it to you to fill in the detail. About Jim's crash in his career. Last thing anyone expected. But I believe now we should have done. Only thankful his parents had gone, so they never had to suffer from the disgrace."

Only you did, Colin thought, looking at the stern old face beside him. Stern and sad; not bitter; he had learned too much of men for that. In any case a fight was a fight and defeat could come to anyone, was sure to come at some time or other. The point was to fight again. And again. As the brigadier had done for his nephew's soul and had lost, again and again.

"They told me afterwards, you see, when I was trying to understand it and made it my business— His old nanny told me he was never to be trusted. He'd take things of hers and if she complained to his mother he'd swear he never touched them and she'd find them again where he'd put them back. So her word was doubted and after a time she didn't complain and the things were not put back."

"Cunning little devil," Colin said, half admiring the ingenuity.

"Exactly. A born devil. Just the same at school. Well, every one takes things they don't own at school. It's universal. You can take them back or fight for them, but unless it gets very bad, money for instance, masters turn a blind eye, don't they?"

Colin nodded.

"He did get into trouble once, but it blew over. He'd bor-

rowed money that time to pay some subscription or other and
didn't pay it, used the money for something he wanted."

"How did he get out of that one?"

"I'm afraid I got him out. He came to me with a good story.
It was the first time. A boy, nearly a young man, his first debt. I
suppose I was flattered he came to the old bachelor uncle. He
was so sorry, I think genuinely so, for the trouble he was causing, so gay when I made fairly light of it, managed to square
his father and so on. He was so damnably lovable."

The old man broke off, staring at the fire.

"It was his last term at school. I paid up and saw his house-
master. He had no illusions. He warned me. He said Jim had
never before done anything he could pin on him, otherwise
he'd have had him sacked. I understood then the various odd
remarks about reliability, truthfulness, things like that in his
reports when my brother showed them to me. I told the man
he should have been more explicit. He said what good would
that have done? He was right, of course. None."

"I didn't know—" Colin began, his own youth, his training
in modern psychiatry, rebelling against such acceptance, such
denial.

"Don't tell me about the advances of medical science, the
trick cyclists and all that," Brigadier Stowden interrupted.
"Jim had a happy childhood, happy and healthy, neither de-
prived nor indulged, parents who were fond of each other and
of their children. I've told you about it precisely for you to
understand that what he became later was fundamental to his
nature, not due to his misfortunes, losing his family in the war
and that."

Colin was silent. His inclination to argue the dead man's
case had passed, his curiosity remained, stronger than ever.

"This—I mean his leaving school for the army—was in 1938.
He was into the war before he was half through normal training and he did well in it." The pride in the old man's voice was
unmistakable, also overlying regret.

"I was proud of him," he said. "I thought service had

knocked the underhand scheming, the lying and the dishonesty out of him. I couldn't have been more wrong."

Colin began to realise what it was costing the old soldier to lift the heavy curtain he had dropped over his nephew's wrongdoings. He tried to stop him, but found he was up against a will far stronger than his own, backed by a far superior weight of experience.

James Stowden had indeed fought bravely and distinguished himself in the field on several occasions. His men adored him. But it was significant, in a war where promotion could be very rapid, that he rose no higher than captain and found himself at the end of it under a colonel who had risen from the ranks of the general call-up.

"He came to see me," the brigadier explained. "Very decent fellow. I won't give you his name. He's retired now, though he stayed on as a regular. Had been trained in his father's business before call-up. Wine trade. That put him on to Jim's fraud. I never really understood it. They should never have let him have charge of the mess. Last thing in the world."

"The colonel found out he'd been embezzling?"

"That sort of thing. Actually changing labels on bottles. Good labels on cheap stuff and kept the difference in the price. Hadn't the sense to realise the colonel'd know the difference, even if the young lads didn't."

"Surely there must have been other people who knew what he was doing?"

"Mess staff, you mean? If there were they lied for Jim. Took a rake-off, possibly. I told you, to the men he could do nothing wrong."

"But was he alone in this fiddle? I thought—"

"There was a friend. Shared the blame. And the punishment. I've sometimes wondered—"

"Yes?"

"If Roy had egged him on, or even had the basic idea. Jim needed money; he always did. The other chap needed it, desperately, we discovered."

"But Captain Stowden had you."

A silence fell between them and rested, deepening. Colin wanted to go, but did not know how to propose it. The disaster he had just heard described was commonplace enough. He had read or listened to similar stories quite often, feeling unmoved by them, except to a kind of contemptuous anger at the over-all stupidity of crime. Especially of petty crime, where the reward was small, the deed nearly sure to be found out, the punishment not worth the risk. But here, in this comfortable, well-maintained, but modest house, in the presence of a grief that would never grow less, for a being who should be con-sidered worthless, but was not, because he had been loved, Colin's natural and trained concern for his own kind filled him, too, with a deep sorrow.

"They don't seem to be able to help themselves," he found himself murmuring and reddened to hear his own voice in such a feeble cliché.

"There's a quotation at the beginning of one of Mauriac's novels," Brigadier Stowden said. "It goes something like *'Il y a des âmes qui Lui sont données'*. Meaning the devil, of course."

He leaned forward to knock out his pipe and said, strongly, "Original sin—I wonder. Not a Catholic, are you?"

"No," said Colin. "Nothing, actually."

The old man said, "Except a doctor. A humanist, I sup-pose?"

"Oh no." Colin was slightly shocked. "Too sentimental. I don't really much like the human race. As a species, I mean. Actually, I shouldn't be surprised if these anti-social psycho-pathic types don't have a chemical basis for their abnormality."

The brigadier was astonished.

"Chemical?" he said, his voice rising. "D'you mean hormones?"

"Bio-chemical. Defective metabolism of some sort. You get a lot of character changes in disease and in accidents. Yes, hormones too, perhaps."

Colin was floundering, reaching the stage at which he did

not really know what he was saying, what he meant, what he exactly thought. To change the subject and find a proper excuse to go, he went on, "After leaving the army what did he do, or would you rather not talk about him any longer?"

"I don't mind talking. I've been thinking of little else since I got the news of his death. What you've just said might be some comfort if it isn't just another lot of hot air. I've had plenty from my own doctor, not to mention the vicar."

He pulled himself upright in his chair.

"Jim came to see me when he got the sack from the army, as he always did, even before he lost his family. We were good friends. He was one of the best casual companions I've ever had. The difference in age didn't seem to count at all. Well, he was very cut up about it, of course. Blamed himself for being found out, chiefly."

"That's typical, isn't it?"

"It was typical of Jim. I won't go into details, but through friends I got him a job in the City. Exporters. Name of Polsen. George Polsen had been at school with me. Had a very bad time in the First War and began making excuses for Him before I was halfway through briefing him on the lad."

"Why?" Colin was mystified.

"Why? Because he thought the Second World War must have unhinged the boy. It had nearly done for himself. He didn't realise the difference. Jim loved every minute of it."

Brigadier Stowden stared at the fire again for a long minute before going on.

"I warned George to keep an eye on him where money was concerned. I told him Jim would be admirable in public relations, staff, customers and so on. George promised and agreed to Jim changing his name. The boy insisted on this. Did it properly, by deed poll. Ivan Totteridge."

"Did he tell you why he wanted to change his name?"

"He did. He told me whatever happened in the future he would never drag my name down again. He never did."

Colin found the brigadier's bright eyes boring into his own

"Was that a chemical reaction, young man?"

"How do I know?" Colin murmured, abashed. And rose to make his escape.

CHAPTER SEVEN

The firm of George Polsen and Springfield Ltd. had offices not far from Tower Bridge and a large warehouse on the other side of the river, further east. The offices were old-fashioned, dark and dirty, very forbidding to Western visitors, who were accustomed to twentieth century chrome fittings and air conditioning. Visitors from the east, on the other hand, found the Victorian furniture and decorations very comforting, very familiar to minds brought up largely on Victorian literature as far as the English side of their education was concerned. Since the bulk of the business of Polsen and Springfield was with the East, the firm had not attempted to change its offices to any extent beyond providing sitting- instead of standing-desks for the clerks, modern filing cabinets and a number of clever machines for recording, typing and so on.

Colin Frost took some time to find the place. He had left Twitbury St Mary the morning after his second talk with Brigadier Stowden, driving back to Brackenfield to leave his car at the hospital and take a train to London. A former fellow medical student was still working, as a registrar now, at their mutual teaching hospital. This man was able to put him up and insisted upon celebrating Colin's arrival with a night on the town. The next morning, while the friend, pale and irritable, went away to the hospital, Colin, with the help of a third cup of coffee, searched the telephone directory and rang up the firm to arrange an interview. Not with George Polsen, who had retired three years before, a female voice told him scornfully. But with Mr Springfield, now the senior partner, who

E

could spare him five minutes just before twelve noon, but he must not be late, she said.

He was five minutes late. Standing in a dim stone hallway, with the names of firms written in long columns on either side of the great doors, Colin took another minute to discover the one he wanted. He had just succeeded when the iron lift door clanged, a tall figure marched towards him, stopped and said, "Are you by any chance Dr Frost?"

Colin said he was and supposed the other was Mr Springfield. "I'm late," he said. "I'm sorry. I don't know this part of London well. I started quite early, but I kept getting misdirected."

Mr Springfield was on the point of saying, "Why on earth not take a cab?" when he realised that the young man in the well-worn suit would not be able to afford it. George Polsen had told him about young Frost. The situation was interesting.

"And I'm a bit early," he said, turning back towards the lift. "So come along up and tell me what you wanted to see George about."

Upstairs in the drab office Colin accepted a whisky and soda and described as shortly as he could his two visits to Brigadier Stowden.

"I must say I missed the case entirely," Springfield confessed. "But after you rang up I got in touch with old George and he gave me a message for you."

"Oh yes?" Colin wondered why the message needed this preamble.

Springfield laughed.

"I've been trying all morning to translate George's remarks into the right language for a serious member of the medical profession. I don't believe I need have bothered."

"Meaning you think I'm *not* a serious member of the—"

"By no means. Meaning I think you can take George's message more or less as it was given."

"Go ahead."

"Well, without the four-letters it was 'tell the bloody young nosey parker I haven't spent fourteen years trying to forget that damned young blackguard, Jim, to have to answer questions about him now'."

Colin grinned. Then he said, "Perhaps you'd be good enough, sir, to give me Mr Polsen's address."

"Not so fast." Springfield looked amused, but resolute. "I take it you're not doing this to sell it to the Press? Can't have the name of this firm brought back into public notice."

"Naturally not. I've told you who I am. We don't sell our patients to the Press or the publishers. That is, most of us don't."

"Very well. But you see why I want to protect my former partner."

"Of course. Perhaps I'd better say that Brigadier Stowden told me how he got the job here for his nephew, under his new legal name of Ivan Totteridge. That's all I do know about his connection with you. I've heard of his criminal past, some of it. And I know about his death, of course, since I treated him. I want information about his time in your firm to find out when and why he knew his own blood group or thought he knew it—"

Mr Springfield stopped him with a raised hand.

"I haven't a clue what you're talking about," he said. "But I think you're genuine and I'm going to send you along to George. Actually take you there. He's in town this morning, at his club. Come along. My car's in our yard, just round the corner."

So Colin found himself, to his surprise and deep amusement, once more eating a plain, well-cooked English lunch in the company of a white-haired, erect, elderly man. Taller and thinner than the brigadier, certainly, but speaking the same language in the same way, in a room where a good many other men of all ages were also feeding and conversing.

"I'm glad you went to Springfield first," the old man told him. "Put you in the picture about the place where young Jim

worked. Old-fashioned, I know. But a lot of our clients from
the East expect us to be like that. If they see us all smartened
up and modernised they think we've been taken over by the
Americans. As so many have, or want to be, in spirit if not in
fact."

"Yes," Colin said, wondering how to get to the point of his
visit.

Mr Polsen wandered on about his business, describing the
many contacts his firm had always had with India, Burma,
Malaya and Singapore. He spoke with knowledge and respect of
the Eastern civilisations and with deep admiration of their arts
and crafts.

The meal over, Mr Polsen ordered coffee and took his young
guest to a secluded corner of a nearly deserted room, where
their conversation was unlikely to be overheard. Colin now
understood that the discourse he had supposed rambling and
verbose was simply a most necessary introduction to what he
wanted to know.

"I hope I have said enough," Mr Polsen began, handing
Colin a cup of steaming black coffee, "—help yourself to milk
and sugar if you take them, my boy—enough to put you in the
picture as to the type of place Jim worked from and the sort of
people he had to deal with."

"I don't quite get the nature of his job, though," Colin confessed.

"No? Business outside your sphere, I suppose?"

"No time for it," Colin answered. "Grants and salaries, too.
No opportunity."

"And never had your nose rubbed in it either, I expect. Was
your father a doctor?"

"Yes. Still is."

Mr Polsen nodded.

"Grants, you said. Or scholarships?"

"A bit of both," said Colin modestly.

"Specialised early, anyhow," said Mr Polsen. "Don't tell me
there wasn't time to widen your knowledge and experience. I

know all that. Same with Jim Stowden. Army far too early. The war. No knowledge of the world. Oodles of charm, you understand. No principles. No idea at all how to manage the commercial side."

"I understand from Brigadier Stowden that he'd never had much idea about money, except that he wanted to use it, a lot of it, and didn't mind where he found it."

Mr Polsen nodded.

"Exactly. I was warned, mind you. Will warned me. Said getting chucked out of the army had completely altered the lad. But it hadn't, you know."

Back to square one, thought Colin. He nodded, waiting for the detail that was so slow in coming. Mr Polsen struck out in a new direction.

"After he'd been with us for two years, apparently working steadily and getting into no sort of trouble, he married my daughter."

Colin nearly groaned aloud. The good English lunch, so much more ample than his usual snatched midday meal, demanded instant exercise. The afternoon was drifting on towards three o'clock. He remembered with a pang, hearing outside the club the footsteps and farewells of those returning to work, that he had intended to reach his own home for tea. Not that he wanted to think of the meal, but he had hoped to complete the drive by daylight and now there wasn't a hope.

"I'm telling you this," said Mr Polsen calmly, watching with amusement the patient, trained attention of his guest, "because it has a very important bearing on what happened next."

Colin sat up straighter, reddening slightly. Mr Polsen went on with his story.

"The marriage had appeared at first to be a great success, but later, Phoebe, my daughter, had begun to show signs of strain. She had found her husband out in several small dishonesties. He was always borrowing money from her, both taking back some of the housekeeping money he gave her monthly out of his salary and also taking part of the small dress allowance or pin money I gave her. But she made no complaint until the row blew up at the office. Neither to me or her mother. In fact she blamed her own carelessness over money matters. She felt it had led him on."

Mr Polsen poured himself out another cup of coffee. Then he said, still looking at the cup in his hand, "He'd been cooking the books in a big way. In spite of the fact that he never had any responsibility for money, as far as we were able to prevent it. But the fact remains that he swindled us out of a quite substantial sum during the three years of his marriage."

"How?" Colin asked, with very genuine curiosity.

"Well, without going into too much detail, which you can get if you want to from the newspaper accounts of his trial, he did it through his wife. He paid cheques into her account, drawn on the firm. He forged my signature and used the firm's stamp. It was easy for him to do this. He could get hold of my regular cheques to Phoebe for her allowance."

"She had a separate account from his?"

"She did, indeed. I made all my children start using bank accounts when they left school. I put them on allowances and made them stick within the limits. Phoebe, poor girl, thought the extra money was to counteract Jim's extravagance. She thought I paid it direct into her account from a sense of delicacy, so she never thanked me outright for these sums. They didn't appear in my private account. They weren't queried in the firm's accounts. Not for three years. Not until Phoebe left him."

"Why was that?"

"She found out that most of the money he took from her was spent on entertaining other women. There were no children to keep her with him. She had no illusions about him by then. So she quit."

"Sensible girl," said Colin.

"I thought so," Mr Polsen agreed. "When she came to tell me what she proposed to do she said she'd have had to leave him sooner if it hadn't been for my extra gifts of money. So then we knew."

"What did you do?"

"Waited till he paid in the next forged cheque, then by arrangement the cashier asked him to see the manager. He agreed, but while the man went off to announce him, he left the bank and ran away to old Will. Always rushed off to his uncle when trouble broke."

"I know," said Colin in a low voice.

"So that was that," said Mr Polsen, a trifle defensively. "We had a special audit, kicked ourselves all round, decided to prosecute. At least, I opted out, but the others insisted."

"Mr Springfield insisted, I expect," said Colin.

A gleam appeared in Mr Polsen's deepset eyes but he only said. "A majority insisted. I wanted to retire as I'd been the one to engage the young scoundrel, but they wouldn't let me at the time."

"When was this?" Colin asked.

"Nineteen fifty-four. Business was tricky then with the break-up of empire. I knew the ropes—the chaps, I mean—at the buying end, so the firm demanded I stay on. Even now they keep my name in it, though my son wouldn't join."

"This was the first time Stowden, I mean Totteridge, had been in court, wasn't it, apart from the army?" Colin asked, when personal reminiscence seemed to be gaining control of the old man's thoughts.

"That's right. Convicted of forgery and false pretences and sent to prison for three years. The army record counted, you see. It wasn't a first offence and there were no mitigating circumstances."

"Just a born crook," said Colin. "Born crook, compulsive liar—"

"What's that?"

"Sorry, sir. Thinking aloud." Colin made a movement to rise, then remembered. "If I'm not taking up too much of your time, there's just one more thing."

"Fire away."

Colin explained Ahmed Patel's mistake and the matter of the diary. Mr Polsen showed the same kind of faintly patronising sympathy that the brigadier had done. Again the Anglo-Indian past presented itself to the young man, this time from a commercial angle. A paternal concern again; no racial feelings; no prejudice, apart from the inbuilt insular British qualified tolerance of all poor bloody foreigners.

"So I wondered if you knew Totteridge carried this note of his blood group and why?" Colin asked at the end of his tale.

George Polsen sat forward.

"I believe I did," he said, with more direct interest than he had shown at any time so far. "Phoebe brought it up when she came to me about leaving the fellow. She was very upset, you see. Never before that let on to any of us how he was treating her. But when we really had all the cards on the table, mine as well as hers, she told me she thought he was going off his head because every now and then he showed her this blood group entry to make sure she hadn't forgotten about it in case of need."

"Did he, indeed?" Colin said, thoughtfully. "Just why did he have this obsession? Did your daughter tell you that?"

"Not that I remember. You'd better ask her."

"Could I? I mean, would she mind? Would you give me her address?"

Mr Polsen was amused.

"You seem to imagine Phoebe is still a poor ill-treated girl with her marriage on the rocks. That was in nineteen fifty-four, remember? She divorced the blackguard, married again very happily a year later, has three children and is now in her middle forties, putting on weight, bless her."

Colin said, with dignity, "You think she would see me, sir?"

Mr Polsen, still amused, promised to arrange a meeting.

This he did, by telephone, before Colin left him. So the next day, having spent another night in London, the latter set off again, this time to an address in Sussex, with a note from her father to introduce him to Mrs Phoebe Lancing, as she now was.

The drive turned out to be a pleasant one when the far-reaching London suburbs were passed. Colin deliberately left the main road as soon as possible and found, as usual, very little traffic to impede him. He enjoyed the quiet rolling countryside of the weald; the pale, late autumn sun, the red and gold of thinning leaves on dark branches, the pools of red and gold below on the wet green turf. He was quite sorry to stop driving, short of the downs, at the Lancings' house on the edge of a small hamlet at a double bend in the road.

It was now about three o'clock in the afternoon. Mrs Lancing was alone and expecting him. Rather wearily he went through his story yet once more, but the audience reaction was strikingly different.

"How perfectly disgraceful!" Mrs Lancing burst out. "Shocking! Horrible!"

"You mean to stab a man in the back when he was driving and cause an accident? Or after he'd been injured in a crash? We don't know which—yet."

"I don't mean that at all! Jim was a criminal. He belonged to the criminal world. He risked his life there all the time, but he took the risk. No. I mean your hospital. That dreadful little Indian! To make such an appalling mistake!"

"It was not Dr Patel's fault," Colin said, suddenly angry. "The fault lies with whoever altered the record in the diary."

Mrs Lancing's face changed. The red flush of anger paled, the scornful lines of her mouth slackened, her eyes grew blank.

"Explain," she said, in a very subdued voice.

Colin began to do so, but suddenly realising his advantage, switched instead to questions.

"I think you knew about Stowden's interest in his blood group?"

"Stowden? Oh, you mean Jim? His name was Ivan Totteridge. I married him as that. But he liked me to call him Jim."

"Didn't you know he had been born James Stowden?"

"No, I didn't. My father only told me that after—after—"

"So you really knew when I mentioned it just now. You do remember his queer obsession with his blood group?"

She did not answer. Colin began to wonder if he ought to go. But when he began to get to his feet, she stopped him.

"No. Wait. I'll tell you. I must, I suppose?"

Colin sat down again. Mrs Lancing's behaviour was unexpected, but hopeful. It reminded him of the patients in hospital who talked at length about unimportant symptoms until the very end of an interview, when they would suddenly produce the whole key to their illness.

His professional patience was rewarded. Mrs Lancing told a strange story. Three years after she had got her divorce, one year after her remarriage, he had arrived without warning. Her first child was only a few weeks old, she was alone in the house with the baby. She understood that Jim had been out of prison for some time, having earned all possible remission of his sentence of three years. During this time he had tried to find her by asking former friends, many of whom refused to see him. He had not approached her father or the firm.

"He came to borrow money again, I suppose?" Colin said.

"No. Not this time. He wanted the blood group. The diary or notebook or whatever he kept it in had been lost. He thought he remembered it, but wanted to check."

"Had you got it?"

"Oh, yes. He made me keep a duplicate note of it. I'd never thrown it away."

"So?"

"So I showed it to him and he copied it into a small notebook—"

"Not a diary?"

"I don't think so. I don't really know. I didn't bother to look. I wanted to get rid of him. He frightened me."

"How d'you mean?"

"Oh, not what you're thinking. He wasn't interested in me at all. Only in getting what he came for. He was different. Thinner—older— Well, I should have expected that. No, different inside himself. Almost—"

"Tell me."

"Almost as if he, Jim as I knew him, wasn't there any more. Is that fanciful?"

Colin looked at her with distaste. Fat and forty, as her father had said. Without imagination, too, or insight. Stupid. No wonder the young Jim Totteridge-Stowden had used her for his fraud. Stupid.

"Not fanciful at all," he assured her gravely. "I would not expect a man of his character to survive a prison sentence without further damage."

"Are you feeling sorry for him?" she asked indignantly.

"No, no. Just medical. No feelings at all."

She looked at him curiously.

"Are you a psychiatrist?" she asked.

Colin was shocked.

"God forbid! I'm rather more than halfway to being a surgeon." Before she could ask any more irrelevant questions he said, "Mrs Lancing, would you be very kind and show me this duplicate note of the blood group? That is, if you kept it? I would have expected him to take it away, or destroy it."

"Oh, no. He asked me to keep it in case he lost it again. Jim all over."

"And you did so?"

"Surely."

She got up at once, went to a desk at the side of the room and after a brief search brought out a visiting card. Her former married name was on one side with a London address. On the other was written, 'Jim's B.G. A.Rh+.'

It was the correct one, he saw. Mrs Lancing had not cheated, planning revenge for those early years of misery. Jim must have copied a correct account. Why had he not remembered it? Easy enough, in all conscience. This had bothered him all along. Why not tell the ambulance man straight off? Easier than directing him to the diary. Afraid he'd get it wrong? Perhaps.

Mrs Lancing had the correct one. If this was indeed the card she had held all the time. It would have been easy, when the ex-convict came asking, to give him a potential, a deferred death. And then replace the real true symbol ready for any inquiry that might, that almost certainly would, follow. Which presupposed the fellow had genuinely forgotten a simple formula that he had always shown the greatest possible interest in preserving. Incredible.

"You knew it yourself, of course," he said, handing the card back to her. "After hearing it so often. You couldn't have forgotten. Or expected him to forget."

"No. I remembered and told him so. But he wanted to see it written down."

"He copied it himself?"

"I told you so."

Colin paused, then said, "Have you by any chance anything written of his?"

Mrs Lancing was affronted.

"Certainly not. The few letters I'd kept, I burned."

Her face was quite white now. With anger, Colin supposed. So he thanked her quietly, said goodbye and drove away. He noticed in his back mirror that she walked out into the road to watch him go.

CHAPTER EIGHT

On the way home Colin considered what Mrs Lancing had told him. He was prepared to take it as a truthful account of her last, brief meeting with Jim. In which case he realised he could take his research a stage further. Two stages, in fact.

Mrs Lancing had said that the discharged convict had himself copied his blood group into a note-book or diary. She had seen him do it. The year of this occurrence was nineteen fifty-seven. The date of the old diary taken from the con man's jacket pocket in the ambulance was nineteen fifty-seven. So presumably it was the one she had seen. He could not prove this, but the fact, if true, was significant.

Also significant was Mrs Lancing's own copy of the blood group, written on her own visiting card. The shape of the 'A' was the usual one, two sloping lines meeting in a point, with a bar across them about halfway down. Since he had seen this card she would not now destroy it. It could at any time be compared with her ordinary writing, if necessary.

So much for Mrs Lancing. Back to the diary. Back to Jim's usual writing, the way he made his capitals. For that, he realised, he would need the brigadier again. But first he must establish that the 'A' in the diary had indeed been altered to a 'B'. He needed to find an expert on writing and on ink. The police could lay on everything, of course, but he still wanted to avoid the police. It would mean giving them the diary and he wanted to keep the little book as his principal excuse for seeing the old soldier again, because the whole matter of the blood group had become more important. So he must know why Jim had given it so much importance; what accident or illness he had suffered that made him develop this mania, why his record of it had been mislaid, for surely he would have told the governor of his prison of it and this man or one of the other prison officers could have provided a copy.

Perhaps his record had in some strange way been truly lost and he could not or would not trust his own memory. Strange, that, over such a simple thing. A, or B, or O were the three most common groups. Too simple, too much alike? Anyway, the chap had gone to his former wife with his unlikely story. Why to her? In the hope that she would give him a false statement by way of revenge so that he could blackmail her afterwards? That would be in line with his later activities. If so, it had failed. Or had it? His own discarded suspicion of Mrs Lancing's good faith returned. She had been very emotional at times during his visit. Was this the painful result of digging up old memories, old feelings about Jim, her love-hate relationship with him. Or was a guilty conscience at work in her? He arrived home in a very sour frame of mind.

In the end he decided to see Brigadier Stowden again, simply and openly to give him an account of what he had done so far and to ask his advice about the next step. It was more than probable the old man had a good knowledge of his nephew's handwriting, even if he had not preserved any of it. It was worth trying, anyway.

So back he went to Twitbury St Mary, where he found the brigadier in a pleasantly agreeable mood.

"You made quite a hit with old George Polsen, it seems," he began, not waiting for Colin to explain the reason for this third visit. "How did you get on with the daughter? A bit heavy on the hand, I always thought. Not too bright, eh?"

"Limited," agreed Colin cautiously. "It was about my interview with her I wanted to see you again, sir."

"Fire away."

Colin explained the blood group developments and complications, to which the old man gave complete and interested attention.

"Let me see," he said when Colin came to an end of his story. "He wrote atrociously. Schoolboy hand, infantile practically."

"I really just want to check if he made the entry himself or if—"

He stopped suddenly.

"Now what's the trouble?" Brigadier Stowden asked.

Colin pulled the diary out of his pocket and handed it across.

"The name," he said. "I forgot to ask her, Mrs Lancing, I mean. What name he was using when he went to see her. That'll be how he managed to get into her house. No, it won't. She said she was alone that day, with the baby. But the name in there now is James Sparks and he wasn't using that till he

left gaol the last time. He was in as Fred Holmes. Before that
he was Ivan Totteridge, wasn't he?"

"No," said the brigadier. "Before that he was Malcolm
Pearce."

"Malcolm — ?"

"Pearce. After he came out the first time, in nineteen fifty-
seven."

"Then how — why — is the name James Sparks written in a
diary dated nineteen fifty-seven? He didn't use this name until
after he was discharged in nineteen sixty-five."

"He may have done. I know he was using the alias Malcolm
Pearce after he left prison in 'fifty-seven. I know he was convicted in 'sixty-three in the name of Fred Holmes. But he did
use other names at different times. James Sparks may well
have been one of them."

"Or possibly whoever it was that changed the blood group
changed the name, too."

The brigadier held out his hand for the diary and looked at
it for several minutes.

"No," he said presently. "There is no sign here that the
name has been changed. It is clearly written, in Jim's own
writing. Pity it's not in block capitals or we could check with
the 'A' in Sparks."

"I suppose it's possible he didn't put in the name at all until
recently. No address so that doesn't help."

"Yes. But anyhow it's in Jim's writing. We shan't get any
further on that. You're trying to establish the whole page
is a fake done by someone who knew him recently. That
won't work. It's his own writing and he could have been using
the name Sparks any time at all in his career."

"Can we prove that, sir?"

Brigadier Stowden grew very red.

"You doubting my word? No. Never mind. Perfectly right.
Let me see. Letters. I've been looking through my papers since
he died. Trying to understand —"

The old man got up abruptly.

"Letters," he was muttering. "Never wrote any recently that I can remember keeping."

He opened a drawer in his desk.

"Photos. Yes. That's it!"

He brought back an enlarged snapshot. It showed two young uniformed smiling subalterns, arm in arm in the brigadier's garden.

"Jim and Roy Waters. Friend of his. Turn it over."

Colin did so. On the back, in capital letters, was written 'A BIG VOTE OF THANKS TO UNCLE WILL'. The 'A' was written with two upright sides and a curved top. The 'B' was similar, a curved line at the top and a straight one at the bottom. The middle line, also straight, joined both uprights. It was identical with the 'B' in the diary.

"This is your nephew's writing?"

"Certainly. I took the snap with the boy's own camera in the garden here. They both came down for a week's leave. Jim sent me the print as his version of a Collins. Roy wrote the usual kind of bread and butter letter."

"That settles it," Colin said. "All I have to do now is prove the correct 'A' of the blood group has been changed by an added line across the base, turning it into a 'B', which is an incompatible group."

"If you take my advice," said the brigadier, "you'll put the police on to that one."

"I think I'll have to do that," Colin agreed gravely. "I'll also tell them what you say about the aliases."

There was a silence between them. Then Colin said, "This Roy Waters. Was he the one mixed up with the army business?"

"Yes. Severely reprimanded, but allowed to finish out his national service. He wasn't staying. He was going in for medicine."

"What happened to him?"

"I never heard. Jim dropped him completely. I sometimes wonder if it was Roy's idea to defraud the mess, rather than

Jim's. His family, Roy's I mean, were not well off. There were grants of a kind by then, but not enough to cover a long course as a medical student. He was keen, though. I expect he made out."

"But he never let you know? Never wrote to ask about Jim?"

"Never. Faded completely. Might never have existed. I sometimes look at that snap and wonder—"

Colin looked at it again. The con man had not changed so very much, he decided. The hair had altered, thinner and greying, the shape of the head and face hardly at all. The casualty had not, of course, smiled. But a young smile—well, it was a pretty universal shape. Both the faces in the photo were lean, clear-cut, healthy. Yes, Jim Sparks, the criminal, was quite recognisable and looked in this photograph entirely innocent.

"There's just one more thing," Colin said. "If I'm not taking too much of your time."

"You said that once before," said Brigadier Stowden testily. "Don't you realise I've retired? Oodles of time—far too much of it."

"About the accident," Colin hurried on. "The one that made him so scared that he got this obsession. What exactly happened?"

"Road crash," answered the old man. "Jeep. After the war. Some exercise or other. Jim was trapped with a deep cut bleeding away where no one could get at it. Nearly died of haemorrhage. Or thought he did. Some delay or other when they did manage to get him out and into the nearest hospital. Thought they could have treated him quicker if he'd had a note of his blood group on him. Don't suppose it'd make any difference."

"Not in the ordinary way it wouldn't," Colin said. "Only if his group was a rare one and they had to send away for it. When would this be, this accident?"

"Oh, just after the war, 'forty-seven, I suppose. He was still abroad."

F

"That might have made a difference."

As there was no answer to this and Colin saw that the brigadier's face was beginning to look grey and tired, he took his leave, with many expressions of thanks for the help he had been given.

"And do keep that photograph locked up somewhere very safe, sir," he said at the moment of parting. "If anyone got to know—"

"Take me for a fool?" said Brigadier Stowden, stiffly.

Colin shook his head without speaking and drove away.

He drove straight to Brackenfield and parked at the hospital. He wanted first of all to give Ahmed Patel a full account of his recent discoveries and after that to take him to the police station to be present when he gave the diary to Inspector Rawlinson.

After some frantic rearrangement of duties the Indian was able to get away for a couple of hours. Rawlinson, not very pleased to see either of the two young men, agreed to give them ten minutes of his time, but forgot about this limit when Colin was fully launched upon his story.

"Brigadier Stowden has the photograph with the writing on the back," he said, "so you can check on the letters from that. The point, as I see it, is that Sparks knew his own group damned well. He'd never stopped worrying over it since the jeep accident. So he wouldn't have put down the wrong one even if his ex-wife had tried to pass it off on him. That is, if there's any truth in her story."

"She told us the same one," said Rawlinson, calmly. "I saw no reason to doubt it."

"*You* saw her? She never said—"

"Why should she?"

"*That*'s why she seemed a bit strange," Colin said, thinking aloud. "Must have thought I was another copper on the same track."

"I very much doubt it," said the inspector, coldly. "Her father told her who you were, didn't he?"

"Well, never mind that. My point is the change must have been made at a date *later* than nineteen fifty-seven, the date of the diary, and *before* the accident on the road here. Nine years. Quite a long stretch to cover."

"Two years were spent inside," Rawlinson reminded him.

"O.K. Seven, then. Made by someone who knew his writing, presumably."

Inspector Rawlinson shook his head.

"Not necessarily. To my mind, if there has been an altera- tion, which I'll have investigated, of course, it was the only way the 'A' *could* have been altered. Anyone could do it who saw how it could be done. He didn't need to know the writing."

He pushed the diary to the side of his desk and sat consider- ing the two grave young faces before him.

"And what do you propose to do now, Dr Frost? I take it Dr Patel is fully occupied at the hospital. What about yourself?"

Colin grinned.

"I shan't be back on the treadmill for another week," he said. "Six days, actually. I thought I'd have a go at finding out what Sparks was doing when he was Malcolm Pearce."

As he hoped Inspector Rawlinson was surprised and showed it.

"After he came out the first time and before he was con- victed as Fred Holmes."

"He had no convictions in the name of Pearce," Rawlinson said quickly.

"I gathered that from the brigadier," Colin told him. "But he didn't offer any other news. He might open up a bit more to you."

"Thanks," said Rawlinson. "Thanks very much. And may I ask how you propose to set about your new bit of research?"

Colin sighed. This heavy sarcasm got neither of them any further. He motioned to Patel, who was only too pleased to escape from an atmosphere he disliked and feared.

"I thought I'd try to look up that girl," Colin said, beginning to turn away towards the door. "Clarice—Field, was it?"

Rawlinson was on his feet, too.

"Clarice Field? Are you telling me you know her?"

"Well, not exactly *know*. Most of us have been to the club occasionally. Not a bad place, in a way. A bit scruffy. Provincial, of course."

He broke off. The inspector was looking angry. Colin was afraid he might have hurt his feelings. He felt he should explain further.

"Naturally, after the inquest, it was obvious the woman in the car must have been Clarice, wasn't it? I didn't have her address so I asked round the chaps and rustled up two, one here and one in London. But you'll have them all, won't you, both of those, at least."

"You'd better tell me which ones you got."

There was no fresh news for him there, the inspector found. His disappointment increased his disapproval.

"The sooner you drop this buffoonery the better, Doctor," he said, reaching his door first and opening it with a jerk. "You may enjoy playing the private eye with people like Brigadier Stowden and his friends, but mind your step in future. Leave the real villains to us. This girl Clarice Field is not at either of those addresses you've got. Pack it in, d'you hear? You can't help anyone, jumping into dangerous places with both eyes shut. What you've brought me may very well exonerate Dr Patel here. Or go some way to doing so. He still acted irresponsibly, didn't he? But I hope it clears him. That's all that concerns you. Don't get under our feet from now on. I warn you."

"That is a very unamiable man, I think," said Patel as they left the police station. "But I think you have done enough, Colin. He was probably right. That knife wound. Very horrible. You must not meet the one who made it. Very dangerous."

Colin laughed.

"I don't intend to. All I want is to find out what Sparks was doing when he was Malcolm Pearce. To discover if anyone he knew then, and probably skinned, could have altered that blood group. Even if his first wife didn't have it in for him, who's to say someone else might not, perhaps even this Clarice, though she always seemed a nice enough girl. But that was professionally, of course."

Patel looked at him sideways.

"Your profession or hers?" he asked gently.

"Her dancing was out of this world," Colin answered in a dreamy voice.

CHAPTER NINE

Though Colin had declared to Inspector Rawlinson that he intended to go on with his search into Jim Sparks's past, he really had no idea how to start. If Clarice Field was not at her usual lodgings, either in Brackenfield or London, and Inspector Rawlinson had declared she had left him, he was up against an obstacle he had no means of removing and he knew it. Help, however, was coming to him from a totally unexpected quarter.

He found, when he reached home, two telephone messages. The calls had been made in the middle of the morning and shortly after four that afternoon.

"He wouldn't give his name, or his business," Colin's mother said. "Just that he understood you were taking a holiday and it was very important that he should speak to you."

"Both times?"

"What d'you mean? Oh, I see. Yes. Same voice, same person. No name. No message."

"Well what am I supposed to do? Ring him up?"

"He didn't say. No number or address, anyway. And no name—as I told you."

"Let's forget him, then."

Mrs Frost smiled at her son and went away to make him a fresh pot of tea. She thought she was very lucky that he still wanted to spend part of his leaves at home. Most of his school and university friends were settled in jobs and had homes of their own. Colin still had a long row to hoe before he got through the sweated-labour stage to become a consultant. All the same she was glad he had not joined his father in general practice, a soul-destroying occupation in many ways since the Health Service broke up the old doctor-patient relationship. Self-service medicine, without the pay-barrier to keep the baskets from being over-filled. There was no future in it, ultimately, in its present form.

"Dad got a surgery this evening?" Colin asked, when his mother reappeared.

"No. He should be in any time now. The new group centre is very nearly ready. He and the partners are getting quite thrilled. They open there the week after next. No more surgeries here. Not even the odd private patient. All the facilities at the centre."

"So they should be," Colin said. He was going on to explain some of the complications of modern diagnosis when the front door bell sent his mother hurrying away. Unpaid receptionist, he thought bitterly. Since the war, at least, and the end of maids living in the house.

Mrs Frost came back almost at once, shutting the door behind her.

"It's the man on the phone," she said. "He's a journalist, I think. But he didn't say so. He still won't give his name. I put him in the surgery."

Colin swore softly, but he went at once to find the visitor.

As soon as he opened the door he knew his mother was right, for he recognised the sole newspaper interloper at the hospital on the night of the accident. He had recognised the thin face, the dark straggle of hair, the spectacles, again at the inquest. Here he was once more.

"Why all the mystery?" Colin asked, standing just inside the room, and staring. He did not allow the other, who was disconcerted, to answer, but went on quickly, "I take it you really want to see me, not my old man?"

"Yes, Dr Frost."

"Mr Frost. Or Colin, perhaps easier. What's your name?"

"Barry Summers. I'm sorry to bother you and the lady—"

"My mother let you in. She took the phone calls, too."

"Pardon. Mrs Frost, then. It's important or I wouldn't—"

"Skip all that. You're here. You're persistent. Get it off the chest."

"It's like this. I was freelance up until that inquest. Now I'm attached to a paper. My editor's interested in night clubs in provincial towns. He cottoned on to the Gregson set-up quite early—"

"He's local himself, I gather?"

"Gregson? Oh no, not really."

"I meant your editor."

"Yes, indeed. *Brackenfield Mercury*."

"Go on."

"Well, I happened to be at the club when Greg found his car'd been nicked and Clary wasn't there any more. So I had a start, see?"

"I do indeed."

"No dice at the hospital—"

"You played that all wrong. In front of the coppers, too."

"I realise now. Doctors are very touchy about the human side."

Colin laughed.

"Come off it! Doctors don't like melodrama souped up out of genuine illness. Most of it isn't dramatic at all, as you ought to know at your age. Never had gastric 'flu?"

"Don't! Please!"

"There's the patient's right to privacy, too. Never mind. Get to the point. Zero at the hospital. Zero plus one or two only at the inquest."

"A little more than that, sir."

"Don't call me 'sir'. Colin Frost is the name."

"Dr—Mr Frost, the inquest was a great help. I looked up all the old stuff, went to the funeral—"

"Did you, now? I didn't see you."

"I took care of that. Got a few hints in the pub. They think you're a long-lost cousin or something out of the old boy's past. That made me go into the family history and so on."

"How far did you get?" Colin asked, eagerly, all his dislike of the intrusion evaporating.

"Army career and disgrace. That came up in the papers at the first court case. Totteridge. Forgery and fraud. Then Fred Holmes and the old woman."

"I haven't come to her yet," Colin interrupted.

"Not? It's quite a story. The trial, I mean. But it's the time in between. The years when he went about as Malcolm Pearce sometimes and Fred Holmes at others."

"Malcolm Pearce!" Colin was really excited now. "Don't tell me you know some real facts about Jim when he was Malcolm Pearce!"

"Well, I wouldn't say *know*, exactly. What I've read—"

Colin seized Barry Summers by the arm and began to pull him towards the door.

"I want to hear every word of it," he cried. "My father will be in any minute now and may want this room, almost certainly will, to write up his visits. We won't turn my mother out of the sitting room. We'll go up to my room. Would you like a cuppa? I'd hardly started tea when you arrived."

"Thanks very much," Barry Summers stammered.

His reception had been so very different from all he had expected that he felt quite bewildered by it. He stood in the hall outside the surgery, hearing Colin's clear voice raised in excited explanation. Mrs Frost murmured a reply he could not catch. Then Colin appeared, carrying a tray in one hand and waving the other towards the stairs.

"My mother has been up already to switch on my fire," he said cheerfully. "That's the beauty of having a G.P.'s wife for your mother. Full range of comfort for any situation, bless her."

Summers nodded and followed his host to the room above, where Colin settled him in the sagging wicker armchair he still cherished from the days of school holidays and the first room of his own. He poured out tea for the journalist and flung a cushion on the floor to sit on himself.

"Now," he said. "Fire away. Malcolm Pearce."

"I remembered the name," Summers began, "in connection with a suicide inquest I had to report. Well, not exactly the inquest. It was Fred Holmes, really. When I was looking up his case. Sorry. That's a bit confusing."

"Understatement of the year," Colin answered. "Start with Fred Holmes, then, and go backwards."

"Right. I was reading up the Holmes fraud case in the papers. The one that got him sent down for two years in 'sixty-three. That led back to the Redfern Hotel burglary, a few months before. One or two of the witnesses said it wasn't his real name."

"No. That was Ivan Totteridge."

"Exactly. The prosecution in the Redfern case was trying to prove he was working in with the gang that staged the burglary at the hotel. But that didn't stick. He'd been discharged in that case. Over the fraud business they dropped the question of aliases. Nothing to do with the fraud or the forgery."

"Where does that get us?"

"Nowhere, officially. But I'd noticed in the Redfern burglary case the other names mentioned. One was Malcolm Pearce. A witness for the defence brought it out. Not the old woman, though she came into it. This other witness swore he wasn't, couldn't be, Ivan Totteridge, because his name was Malcolm Pearce. A very unconvincing witness. In cross-examination she broke down and said one or two highly incriminating things.

Pearce or not Pearce she recognised the chap all right, though she went on swearing he wasn't Totteridge or Holmes. The defence ought never to have produced her."

"So you got hold of her afterwards, I suppose?"

"After the inquest, yes."

"Inquest? No, don't tell me! You started with an inquest. When?"

"Nineteen sixty-one."

"Two years *before* the Fred Holmes trial?"

"That's what I mean. The name Malcolm Pearce came into the inquest. Then when I was looking up the Fred Holmes trial, there it was."

Colin thought this over.

"What had Pearce to do with the inquest?"

"According to a friend of the dead woman he'd been a friend of hers, a very great friend. But her sister denied it."

"Ah."

Barry Summers sipped his tea and waited. After a few seconds Colin said, "You have the sister's name and address, I hope?"

"Name, yes. A Miss Gertrude Short. Present address, no. Left the old one after the sister died."

"You drove her away, I suppose? Invasion of privacy—"

"Now look here!" Barry put down his cup and stood up, red-faced, indignant.

Colin laughed. He scrambled to his feet, put his hands on the other's shoulders and pushed him back into the armchair, which tilted, creaking dangerously.

"I never even spoke to her at the court," Barry protested.

"O.K. I believe you. But you must have tried to see her recently or you wouldn't know she'd moved."

"I did that. And I've made a few inquiries. Pubs, neighbours. Nix. I'm stuck."

Colin considered again. Then he asked, "Was this address you went to the one given at the inquest or the one given at the Fred Holmes trial?"

"Inquest. It wasn't the sister at the trial. Or the neighbour. Quite a different woman."

"Bit of a lad, wasn't he?" Colin murmured, thinking hard.

"I wondered if you might have gathered a few details from the old uncle."

"Brigadier Stowden told me," Colin said firmly, "that his nephew, Jim, always went to him for help when he was in trouble, but not otherwise. He knows nothing whatever about Malcolm Pearce."

Summers was not convinced.

"Sure he doesn't? What about the inquest? The coroner wanted to question Malcolm Pearce, but he was never found."

"So presumably he didn't consider himself in trouble and didn't run to Uncle Will that time. Cold-hearted devil, wasn't he?"

"Or scared of coming out into the open. I don't blame him, he'd already been in the nick, once. Anyway the police didn't bother to look for him, obviously. Breaking hearts is not illegal."

The conversation flagged. Colin explained that his leave was nearly up and that once back at work he would only have alternate weekends during which he could continue his research. Apart from this, Inspector Rawlinson had warned him off trying to sort out the con man's enemies. The woman, the sister of the suicide, this Gertrude Short, might have something to tell if they could find her. Or rather, if Barry Summers could find her.

"I'll go on trying," the journalist promised, looking disappointed. "I'd rather hoped you'd be able to get Brigadier Stowden interested enough to help me."

"How?"

"He just might know something about the suicide. If the Short woman knew her sister's fancy man had an important uncle—"

"Old Stowden told me his nephew had promised never to bring him into his troubles again."

"But did he say he never *had*. I thought you said he always ran to him for help."

"Not publicly, he hadn't."

"All right. So this wasn't public either. That doesn't mean Stowden never knew anything."

Colin resented so much pressure, also so much disrespect for a distinguished figure, though he half admired the other's persistence.

"I'll write to him," he promised. "He may not answer, but I'll risk it. That's as far as I'll go at present. I've been all out on this case since it happened. I want a few days to think it over."

Privately he knew he must take a few days' real rest before being caught back into the endless work at the hospital. So Barry Summers had to leave, not altogether pleased with his lengthy interview. He had given away most of his own actions, he realised, for very little return from Colin Frost. He also understood how their aims diverged, a very real and possibly frustrating position. If Colin could prove that his Indian buddy's part in the con man's death was forced upon him by another attempted murder and therefore that his fault was secondary and hardly blameworthy, the young surgeon would be satisfied. He would drop the case. Whereas his own ambition was to play a major and proclaimed part in the arrest and conviction of a man who had attempted murder by the cruder method of the knife. A method that would appeal far more to the journalist's editor than the other. People understood knives but not blood groups.

While Barry Summers travelled, sad and dispirited, towards Brackenfield, Colin cleared his own obligation by writing to Brigadier Stowden. In his letter he stated, hopefully, that he thought the latter would like to know the latest position about the blood group findings. Also he wanted to report on his own activities. He described his meeting with Inspector Rawlinson, only leaving out the detective's warning not to search for the criminal specialists. He also recounted Barry Summers's appearance and the rather dim light it threw on Jim as

Malcolm Pearce. Could the brigadier possibly add to that? They would both be very pleased if he could help them.

After reading the letter over Colin cut out the last sentence. He did not really see Uncle Will, obliging as he had shown himself, setting out deliberately to help a minion of the evil witch, publicity. It meant copying out a substantial page of writing, but Colin did it and felt safer afterwards.

Just before he went back to Brackenfield at the end of his leave he had a letter from the brigadier. In this the old soldier made no reference whatever to Barry Summers, his discoveries or his possibly usefulness. Jim had mentioned once or twice that he was calling himself Pearce since his release from prison. He had told his uncle he had a job and was earning good money, but did not say what the job was. He gave no address at any time for the next four years and very little news except that his wife had divorced him and married again, which naturally he knew from the papers, apart from what George Polsen told him. In fact, he had begun to think Jim had settled down at last when the first Fred Holmes case broke. Jim had been charged as an accomplice of burglars, but had been cleared and discharged. Shortly afterwards he had been held on a new charge, of forgery and false pretences, the victim being an old woman who had been an unwilling witness in the first trial. This time Jim got two years.

Colin considered sending Uncle Will's letter to Barry Summers but decided against this course. Quite apart from the need to keep the old man secure from further shock, Colin did not want to risk his growing friendship with someone from a world and time so entirely different from his own. His father, grandfather and great-grandfather had followed science, medicine and the art of healing. The Stowdens had pursued the art of war. He found the brigadier's attitudes, cast of mind, conventions and myths both strange and fascinating. Living history, he told himself, not yet recognising his own inherent attitudes, cast of mind, conventions and myths.

So there the matter rested for nearly three weeks, when

Colin had a telephone call from Summers, asking to see him in private.

"I don't want to be thrown out of the hospital again," he said, when Colin invited him to the residents' quarters.

"You won't be. At least—"

Barry was such an obvious member of his profession, as recognisable as any game dog or collie.

"Meet me at the King's Arms at the corner, then, and we can walk."

"Not the pub. They know me. Front gate of the hospital."

"Whatever you say."

Colin welcomed the exercise though he did not expect any news of importance.

He was wrong. Barry had important news. He had located Miss Gertrude Short, had made actual contact, knew where she lived, had even secured a promise from her that she would agree to meet the surgeon who had attended the last hours of Malcolm Pearce.

"How in the world did you bring off all that?" Colin asked, when the story came to an end.

"Find her, d'you mean?"

"Yes, find her. You're stalling. I want to know and you're bloody well going to tell me."

Already he anticipated some revolting move. It was about what he feared, he decided. Barry, using his journalist's imagination linked with his previous knowledge, from her reported answers, of Miss Short's likely behaviour, had first set about discovering where his sister had been buried, next the grave in a public cemetery and lastly, from the attendant there, whether he knew if the grave was ever visited.

"Regular, you see," Barry explained. "On a Saturday morning, once a month, with flowers. It was first time lucky for me. There she was. Unmistakable."

"You make me retch," said Colin roughly.

"Whyever? Don't you want to see her? Ask her things? She's the only one who knows."

"Who did you tell her you were? I bet you lied."

Barry was annoyed, affronted, but held back his anger. The story he wanted, was determined to get, would be withheld from a journalist, he was sure, but would, just as surely, be laid before a doctor. So he said nothing, looked as hurt and resentful as he felt and trudged along beside Colin in his rather thin, unsuitable shoes, hoping that much-needed exercise would improve his companion's temper.

Naturally Colin gave way in the end. He was just as anxious to take his investigations further as Barry was to secure his help. He dared not refuse this opportunity. Miss Gertrude Short sounded harmless enough, but clearly she had been devoted to her sister. In which case she must have been Jim's enemy, even if a passive one. It was an enemy who had attempted his murder, an active enemy. He must know if the suicide's sister had been capable and willing to pass into that role.

CHAPTER TEN

Miss Gertrude Short lived in a small semi-detached suburban house in a road of similar houses near the Kingston by-pass. She worked all day in the City of London office where she had spent the whole of her business life, having risen from the lowest rank of typist to that of confidential secretary to the managing director.

She had never married, not so much because she did not have the looks or the temperament to attract the attention of men, but chiefly because she had never understood that it was necessary to cultivate these attributes if she hoped to achieve anything. It was not that she wished to avoid marriage. All her life she nourished romantic ideas and hopes with a stream of books and films in which she adopted the part of the heroine. This kept her in a cheerfully anticipatory frame of

mind, so that she did not notice the years slipping past nor
calculate the diminishing prospects of success. She simply continued to wait.

Colin met the journalist by arrangement at the end of the
road at eight o'clock one evening. It was not a very convenient
time for the registrar. It meant postponing his dinner and he
always found himself very hungry at the end of a busy afternoon, whether spent in Out-patients or in the operating
theatre. But he understood why Miss Short had chosen eight
o'clock. She wanted to get her own evening meal out of the
way and yet keep the interview to an hour that no one could
accuse of dubious meaning.

Barry Summers was punctual. As he and Colin walked up the
road he explained Miss Short's circumstances.

"Typical dyed-in-the-wool secretary," he said. "Absolutely
truthful, but holds back everything she doesn't want you to
know. I admire her, but I got stuck over her sister. That's
where you come in."

"I'm not going to deceive her," Colin said, recoiling from
the hint of conspiracy. "I shall tell her exactly what I want
to know and leave it to her whether she comes across or
not."

Barry looked sour, but said nothing.

The door was opened by a girl, whose youth, when she had
tossed her streaming hair back from her face, was clearly revealed.

"We've an appointment with Miss Short—" Barry was beginning, when a voice from behind the girl said briskly,
"That's all right, Susan. I'll cope," and a middle-aged, square-
faced woman took the other's place quietly but firmly and said,
"Will you come in, please."

The two men followed her into a pleasantly furnished small
living room at the back of the house, with a view of a small,
neat garden. The girl had melted into one of the front rooms
as they passed down the hall.

"I have two resident students," Miss Short explained.

"Rather inquisitive, but reasonably clean. I could not have kept the house on alone."

"Forgive me," said Colin, dropping into Miss Short's somewhat formal speech, "but that would be after your sister's death?"

Miss Short bowed her head. Her face was quite composed, but Colin noticed that her fingers shook. Barry got up from his chair.

"I haven't introduced Dr Frost properly yet, Miss Short," he said. "He has come all this way from Brackenfield specially to see you. After hearing what you told me the other day. I'm sure you would rather talk to him alone."

Colin passed him the key of his car.

"Wait for me, Barry," he said. "I won't keep Miss Short very long."

The journalist left the house swiftly, avoiding the students, who both erupted into the hall as he opened the front door. Colin and Miss Short heard him call goodbye to them as he escaped.

"Students, did you say?" Colin asked lightly and laughed.

"That's what they call themselves," answered Miss Short briefly.

"Well now. I think Mr Summers told you why I've come."

"Mr Summers told me about the death of that—that *murderer*," said Miss Short, her voice no longer calm, indifferent, but filled with such a passion of hate that Colin was shocked.

"You mean—" he stammered.

"I mean that he brought about my sister's death as surely as if he had shot, stabbed or poisoned her. He knew her nature. He knew how she felt about him, how she had suffered in the war. He was utterly callous, brutal, wicked—murderous."

Colin waited a few seconds for her to recover from this outburst. When she was calmer he asked again for more detail, for a clearer account of what had happened. With many hesitations and digressions he was able at last to build up a fairly coherent story.

G

Miss Short had had one sister, younger than herself, no brothers. The sister had married during the war, having been in the WAAF. Her husband, a pilot, was killed. She continued in her war service and after the war until the middle fifties. Then, their parents being both dead and the old home given up, she had left the WAAF to keep house for her sister.

"Here?" Colin asked. "Where you are still living?"

"Yes. She wanted me to stay. She knew I was settled, that it would be difficult for me to be uprooted again. She said all this in the note she left."

Miss Short, it appeared, had not been called up for national service. Her firm was essential to the war effort and she had been declared indispensable. This was not surprising when all other staff of her age had left.

"So you were living here together when your sister met Malcolm Pearce? She had not remarried?"

"Certainly not." Miss Short looked slightly shocked. "There were no children. I think she always regretted that, though of course it was really a blessing. And anyway, how could she have started a family when she was a serving officer?"

Only too easily, Colin thought, disagreeing with every word Miss Short had spoken. But time was getting on and he had heard nothing useful yet. He began to doubt he ever would, but his patience was in the end rewarded.

"Mabel met this man quite by chance," Miss Short went on. "And unlucky, an evil chance. She told me he had helped her with her shopping bag. A perfectly trivial thing, but I'm sure he arranged it. He saw a likely victim and laid his plot to trap her."

Miss Short's inner life was coming to the surface. The more she told of her sister's infatuation, the more Colin felt he was hearing an extract from an old-fashioned magazine story. When it came to the moment of betrayal or rather to poor Mabel Banks's confession of her own stupidity, Miss Short suddenly switched back to the totally competent confidential secretary she really was and always had been.

"Poor darling, she thought he was going to marry her. He'd been through the war himself, as she had, though not in the same service. His was the army. He told her he'd been invalided out. They weren't too old. She was only thirty-four when they met. That was in 'fifty-seven. He kept her on the hook for three years. She gave him all her savings. The war gratuity she'd kept untouched. She did a little part-time job in a children's school, pre-primary play group sort of thing. Keeping house for me didn't take up all her time, you see, and she was fond of children. He got those wages out of her, too. I believe he practically lived on her for those three years."

"I doubt it. He had very expensive tastes. Did you never suspect him?"

"*I* did, but what could I do? Mabel wouldn't hear a word against him. Now I think of it, there were times when he didn't show up for weeks at a time. Mabel said he was travelling for his firm."

"He pretended to have a job, then?"

"Oh, yes. Very grand about it. Had all the jargon."

"He would. He'd been in business as well as in the army. Thrown out of both."

Miss Short considered this.

"If only I'd allowed myself to make inquiries. Or asked for help. But Mabel was so happy. Right up to the end she was in a dream of happiness. That was why—"

A dream of happiness which you shared, Colin thought. You shared the happiness that had never come your own way. And the guilt, the disillusion, when it came to an end. Or perhaps only the guilt. Illusion was too essential to her very existence to risk extinguishing it.

Miss Short continued her story. In 1960, after another absence, longer than any before, Malcolm Pearce had written to Mabel. He was to be sent abroad on business, he did not know for how long. He might have to be resident abroad permanently. He was heartbroken, but it was goodbye. He

thanked her for all she had done for him, all she had been to
him. He would never forget her.

"That must have opened your sister's eyes?" Colin said.

"No. It didn't. It opened mine, though. I tried hard to
persuade her to forget the whole thing. She said she belonged
to him. It was the first time I suspected—"

Incredible, Colin thought. But remembered in time that
Miss Short had been brought up in a world of respectable
sniggers and innuendo and false values. He swallowed his
indignant unbelief.

"She refused to pack it in, get him out of her hair?" he said
instead.

Wincing, Miss Short agreed.

"Worse," she said. "She began to try to find his firm, to get
his address."

"But he never let her know where he lived?"

"Oh, yes. In fact she'd been there with him—often, she told
me. Rather dingy lodgings, she described them, near Shepherd's Bush. She would never tell me, exactly. But he'd left
there. She said his landlady told her he'd gone away, abroad."

"So she concluded he really meant what he'd written in the
letter."

"I think she believed it from the start. It was just grief she
felt. She kept telling me he'd given her up for her own sake,
because he couldn't provide for her, or his firm didn't want
him to have a wife. Some nonsense of that sort."

Miss Short was all commonsense now. All contempt for
Malcolm's lies.

"What really stopped her getting over it?" Colin was still
puzzled. "Why didn't she just accept what she thought were
the facts? She'd accepted them before when her husband was
killed."

"That would only make it more difficult, wouldn't it? I
mean the unfairness. Cheated *twice* by fate."

Back to romance, Colin groaned inwardly. As if fate was
ever fair? What *was* fate, anyway?

Aloud he said, "You were going to tell me what happened to drive her over the edge."

Miss Short bent her head. "She saw him."

"*No!*"

"Oh, yes. I told you he was utterly callous. He was in lodgings not a mile from where he'd been before, as far as I can make out. He frequented the same pubs. So when Mabel went visiting the haunts where they'd been happy together—just to remind herself of what she'd lost—morbid, I know, but very natural—it was only a matter of time before she ran into him. With another woman, of course."

Clear enough now, the pathetic, pointless, wasteful, self-indulgent suicide. Colin understood. A few visits to the doctor, a generous supply of soothing poison, an easy finish. But a lasting bitterness for the surviving sister, whose secretarial excellence had been quite unable to cope with an all too common situation when it appeared in her own home and family.

Turning away from the death, Colin said, "Did Malcolm Pearce attend the inquest?"

Miss Short was surprised and rather shocked.

"Oh, no," she said. "His name hardly appeared. If I could have brought her death home to him I would have gone to the police. But she told me nothing, except that she'd seen him, she knew now he'd been deceiving her, his name was not Malcolm Pearce and I was never to speak of him again, to her or anyone else.

"I respected her wishes," said Miss Short, and added, "Not that I anticipated she would act as she did. I never anticipated that."

"I don't quite understand," Colin said, "why you decided you couldn't pin her motive for suicide on Malcolm Pearce. Did she really never tell you his address? When you both accepted him as genuine and it seemed likely he would marry your sister?"

"No. Never while she lived. But I found it among her

things, later. I went there, after she died. Dingy lodgings, like she said. The woman in the house said she'd never had a lodger called Pearce. I described him and Mabel, too. But she insisted I was mistaken. It would have been my word against hers and that was the first time I'd gone there. Never while she was alive."

Colin nodded.

"Naturally you wouldn't suspect he was already known to the police, under other names. I think he used Pearce only to Mrs Banks. That reminds me. How did she know he'd changed his name when she saw him again by chance? Did she tell you that? It might be very important."

"She heard the other woman call him Fred. Fred, darling, to be exact. Before that she'd been going to speak to him. She was overjoyed to see him. Thought he must have just got back unexpectedly and hadn't had time to get to her. She trusted him still, you see, absolutely."

"So it was a tremendous shock to hear the other woman speak like that to him?"

"Yes. It opened her eyes all at once, she told me."

"Don't you think her eyes were about half open already? I mean his name might have been Fred as well as Malcolm. The woman might have been a relation, sister, cousin or something. She jumped to a conclusion—the right one, of course—pretty smartly, didn't she?"

Miss Short agreed reluctantly.

"Perhaps. Yes. When he said such a final goodbye to her—by letter, too. The trip abroad was a very lame excuse. I thought so myself, as I told you, but dared not say so to her. She was not a fool. Yes, I think she must have had her suspicions."

There seemed to be nothing more to say. Colin took down the address in Shepherd's Bush in case Inspector Rawlinson would find it useful. It seemed unlikely that the London police had not traced it before the Fred Holmes trial, but they did not seem to have got his connection with Mabel Banks and her tragic end.

Colin realised, however, that he had not yet approached the question of the blood group. He did so now. Miss Short's answer was unexpected.

"Didn't I read about this in the paper?" she said, returning to her most sensible, efficient manner after a short spell of eye-wiping and nose-blowing. "It caught my attention because of the fuss Malcolm always made about a little diary he had. He thought he'd lost it one time out of the inside pocket of his jacket. In our house, too."

Miss Short blushed slightly.

"I couldn't help wondering why he'd taken his jacket off. It was not in the summer it happened. We found it, of course. At least Mabel did. She didn't say where. I believe it was in her own bedroom."

"Did she say why he was worried about losing it?" Colin asked, steering Miss Short away from her embarrassment.

"Oh, yes. His blood group. Such an extraordinary thing, I remembered it. I couldn't help wondering—"

"You were perfectly right. Same man."

Colin explained the cause of the obsession and the result of the false entry, watching Miss Short carefully as he did so.

"I suppose you don't remember the group written down in the diary?" he asked, in a very matter-of-fact voice.

"Why should I? I never saw it. Mabel never told me. Why do you ask?"

The negatives tumbled out too fast, Colin thought. Miss Short was altogether too emphatic. But there was nothing more he could say. He thanked her, apologised for keeping her so long and left the house. He looked back over his shoulder once or twice as he walked away, but though he caught a glimpse in one of the front windows of streaming hair and black-framed eyes, Miss Short, unlike Mrs Lancing, was not watching his departure.

Barry Summers, lolling in the passenger seat of Colin's car with his eyes shut, seemed to be taking a short nap. But he straightened up quite briskly when Colin pulled open the driver's door.

"Any luck?" he asked, as they drove away.

"Yes and no. By the way, she still lives in the house she shared with her sister. Never moved away, she says."

Barry stared.

"Well, I'll be— Then she must have given a wrong address at the inquest. How could she?"

"Perhaps stayed with a friend for a bit and gave that address."

"You're right. That must be it. I've got it! Mrs Banks killed herself at her friend's house. The friend who gave evidence. Miss Short went there on getting the news and stayed over. How's that?"

"I thought you said you'd looked up the inquest. You'll have to check again."

Colin went on to describe his interview in detail and added, "Another deadly enemy but too distant in time. Jim knew his blood group, written on his heart, like Calais—"

"Like *what*?"

"Broody Mary and all that. No? Never mind. I can't believe he wouldn't notice an alteration, wouldn't have checked the entry sometime in all the years before his death. I don't believe Gertrude Short ever saw him again. I don't see how she could."

"O.K. Registered as an enemy, but not suspected. Keep her on the list but pass on to the next."

"And who may that be?"

"The old trout in the second court case against Fred Holmes."

"Who was she?"

"I'll look her up and let you know. If you're still interested. You can drop me here, if you will."

"I thought I was driving you back to Brackenfield?"

"You were, but I've changed my mind. 'Bye for now."

It was a week before Colin heard from Barry Summers. This

time it was to tell him that a certain Mrs Helen Woodford-Smyth would be interested to see him. She lived in a private hotel in Kensington and was free any morning of the week, except Sunday, between eleven and twelve noon.

CHAPTER ELEVEN

It was a fortnight later still before Colin was able to take advantage of the journalist's information. But when he found he was free to leave Brackenfield for forty-eight hours, he got in touch with Barry and proposed to drive him to London.

"You'd better ring the old girl up and tell her we're coming, hadn't you?" he suggested.

"O.K. If I say we'll pick her up in a car she'll probably jump at it. Her present place isn't a patch on the Redfern."

Barry rang off without waiting for Colin's answer. However, they had already fixed a time for leaving Brackenfield and would have a couple of hours' drive during which they could exchange information and work out a plan of action, so Colin made no effort to renew contact until the following Saturday morning.

"Where exactly are we going?" he asked, when he was free of the town traffic and moving out along the London road.

"Still in Kensington—just. Calls itself a hotel but really it's a guest house. I think they're all permanent. A weird collection. I imagine Mrs W-S lost some of her capital when she knew Jim Sparks."

"Who didn't? Did she tell you why she left the Redfern?"

"No. The manager did, though. Still believes she had something to do with the raid, but as he was responsible for letting Jim have a room there, he was helpless. The police might have picked on him, too, as another conspirator."

"I'm not very clear—"

"Let her tell you herself. It makes quite a tale."

It certainly did, when Mrs Woodford-Smyth was finally induced to revive her very painful experience. Which she did in the early afternoon, sitting in Colin's car, parked at the edge of the Serpentine, staring before her at the water and the ducks swimming there.

Before that, the two young men had worked long, patiently and with determination to bring this about.

Barry went into the guest house to find Mrs Woodford-Smyth. She came out, overdressed in a long, shabby fur coat, a flowered and spangled violet-coloured hat, high-heeled, black patent leather shoes splayed in the toe section, a black patent leather handbag and violet coloured gloves. When she saw Colin, in a tweed jacket and grey flannel trousers, his hair ruffled by the wind, standing beside his very old car, she recoiled in evident dismay. But Barry, who expected this re-action, guided her forward, introduced her and said, "Dr Frost and I would like you to have lunch with us, if you will. We are rather late now to have our talk and bring you back here for lunch. Traffic holdups, you know."

As she still looked disappointed, bewildered, inclined to be angry, Colin said, "I thought that restaurant in the park, near the lake, you know where I mean? Looks out at the water."

It would be very costly, he thought inwardly, panicking a little. He had been there only once before, when the girl of the moment, whom he had ditched soon after because she was far too expensive, had insisted upon being taken there. It had been wonderful on a warm June evening, apart from the hole in his wallet. It would not be wonderful today, on a dull late November morning with the leaves nearly all down, but it might pay off and Barry had agreed to go halves over feeding their guest.

Mrs Woodford-Smyth brightened. Saturday lunch at the guest house was always dreadful. The breakfasts there were always meagre. Greed, anticipation and the company of two young men, however scruffy, made her so excited she even spoke the exact truth as they drove away together.

"I've never been there," she said. "Though I often take a bus to the park in the summer and walk and sit under the trees. It wasn't built, the restaurant I mean, when I first lived at the Redfern. You know I used to live at the Redfern? So convenient for the shops. Not like my present home. But what does it matter when one can't afford to buy anything."

Colin glanced sideways at her. She was taking up rather more than the front passenger seat; the fur coat tended to droop over the controls. She had approached the right mood too quickly. Glancing in the back mirror as he waited for the traffic lights to change so that he could enter the park, he met Barry's eyes and raised his own eyebrows inquiringly. Barry shook his head.

The lights went green, Colin drove on. Mrs Woodford-Smyth gathered her coat round her as he pushed it away from the gear handle and remained in silence until they stopped in the car park of the restaurant.

The meal was a great success. Under the shabby coat Mrs Woodford-Smyth's violet-coloured wool dress was well-cut and simple, only marred by too great a profusion of costume jewellery. At a distance the general effect of Kensington dowager was only very slightly spurious.

She had taken control of the party as soon as she was inside the restaurant, attracting the immediate attention of the head waiter, telling him, "Three, near the window, if possible. The view is so delicious."

Her smile of familiar pleasure was wonderful. The head waiter felt he ought to remember her but could not. However, an important lady, with her grandson and his friend. Students, perhaps. The head waiter had not been in England very long.

Colin began to understand a little about Mrs Woodford-Smyth. At the end of the expensive meal, which she ate with considerable relish, he understood still more. The poor old thing was half-starved. Probably paying far more than she ought, simply for an address, though that was patently misleading; in any case, far too little for her food. He remembered that she had left no message to say she would be out for lunch, so he reminded her of this.

"I go out so often," she answered readily, smiling at him. "I only let them know if I shall be in."

As he thought, she must be on half cover, demi-pension. Breakfast and dinner. Toast and tea, then a gaping void until the evening. He despised her stupid snobbery, but he felt sorry for her all the same.

In the car park after the meal Barry said goodbye to Mrs Woodford-Smyth. He had a business appointment, he explained.

"Not me," Colin said. "I was hoping you would let me ask you a few questions—as a doctor. I think Barry has explained my interest."

"I hardly understood a word he said," she answered gaily. The wine she had drunk had deepened the colour of her face to a faint lilac that clashed unhappily with the violet dress and hat.

"Never mind. We'll start at the beginning again," Colin told her. He began to fear that the difficulty now would be to stop the flow, not promote it.

But he was wrong. When, after cruising round for a while, he saw an empty place among the cars at the Serpentine and dashed into it, Mrs Woodford-Smyth sat perfectly silent for several minutes, while the lilac tinge faded from her cheeks, the heavily-powdered jowl dropped lower and a few indrawn breaths made Colin fear she was about to break down in tears.

"You need not tell me about Fred Holmes," he said, to help her and save them both embarrassment. "I happen to know his uncle and have heard a lot from him about the life Holmes led."

"I was utterly deceived," the old woman answered, clutching her handbag so hard that it shook against her knee. "Voice, manner, clothes, everything. A mountebank, a charlatan, a *criminal.*"

"No," said Colin. "Genuine enough. Army family, third

generation. Criminal, if you like. Yes, criminal. He certainly broke the law."

"He broke more than the law," she answered tartly. "He broke hearts and he broke fortunes. But you say he was born a—a gentleman. I was not altogether deceived by him, then."

Not by Jim, Colin thought; mainly by her own pretensions and desires. He would have to go carefully. Perhaps if he had been able to establish Jim as a cunning, money-grubbing gigolo, which in this case he must have been— Too late. Better leave it to Mrs Woodford-Smyth.

She was thoroughly roused, now. The never-sleeping resentment took charge.

"It all began with his doing me a little courtesy," she said. "I had come out without my umbrella. I was walking in Kensington Gardens as I often do. I have been a very lonely woman, Dr Frost, since my husband died. Well—to be exact—since he left me, six years before he actually died. The usual story, you know—his secretary. I never divorced him, but of course after his death I got very little; only what the law demands."

She broke off, sighing, not looking round at Colin, but still staring ahead at the lake.

He sighed too, inwardly trying to find some way of bringing the story forward to her association with Jim.

"You came out without your umbrella," he reminded her, in desperation.

"Yes. And naturally it began to rain. And the next thing there he was, opening a big black man's umbrella over me and saying, 'Please let me offer you shelter. Where do you wish to go?' Delightfully put, I thought. He took me all the way to the High Street Underground, said that was where he had to go himself, found me a taxi and saw me off."

"Learning your address as you gave it, of course."

"I suppose so. Yes. I suppose it was all deliberate."

"And then?"

"Oh, we met again. Inevitably. At longish intervals. Nothing to make me suspicious. I thought I'd found a friend. He was youngish, but not a boy. You do understand that, don't you?"

"Of course."

She would have described herself at that period as youngish but not a girl, Colin thought. It was going to take a very long time to establish the relationship that grew up between them. He decided it would be unbearable to listen to it told in Mrs Woodford-Smyth's idiom. So he said, in a very matter-of-fact voice, "How long was it before he began asking you for money?"

She turned to look at him then, with a curious kind of relief showing in her small, faded eyes.

"About three months, I think. By then—by then, Dr Frost, I was not really my own mistress."

A neat way of explaining that by then she was Jim's. Colin quite admired her for it. He kept silent and the whole commonplace, sordid affair was laid before him.

At no point in their association had Jim appeared to be other than reasonably prosperous, reasonably well dressed and fed. He needed the money, he always told her, for setting up branches of his business in different towns in the midlands and north. This accounted for his fairly frequent absences from London. At least he said he was away, but she thought now that he was simply working for the gang he was associated with.

His criminal role turned out later to have been suspected for some time, but never proved. He made contact with a potential victim, visited her house, got to know her and her surroundings, her possessions and her income and then thieves would raid her and collect the valuables he had reported. In none of these cases did suspicion fall upon him directly. He never took money from these women nor attempted any kind of intimacy. Often he was accepted as a friend of the family, played golf with the husband, took adolescent children to the theatre. But he had been a friend. Under a great variety of names, a friend, until after the burglary. Then the relationship lapsed. Gradually. The insurance company paid compensation; in the excitement Jim's absence was scarcely noticed. The victims recovered from their losses. Jim and his associates prospered.

All this was explained to Mrs Woodford-Smyth when the police were trying to implicate Jim, as Fred Holmes, in the burglary at the Redfern. For her case was rather different. Jim must have realised at an early date, Colin decided, that Mrs Woodford-Smyth's copious jewellery was all fake, not a real pearl or diamond in the lot. But the Redfern Hotel was another matter. A good many of the residents were by no means fake. Barry had reported on this. They might be living on reduced dividends, on annuities, even on capital, but they had, in many cases, kept their valuables as a last resource. Their rings, bracelets and necklaces survived from happier days. The old men had their shirt studs, tiepins, gold watches, silver cigarette boxes. Even their medals. Perhaps some valuable porcelain from the Far East. Jim, visiting his elderly mistress at discreet intervals, had no doubt made himself familiar with these treasures and with the geography of the hotel.

"I ought to have suspected something when Fred began to spend weekends at the Redfern," Mrs Woodford-Smyth said sadly. "He told me he had really left London and could only come up at weekends, occasionally. He asked me to book him a room on the ground floor, because it was cheaper than the first floor, where my room was."

"I didn't know there were any ground-floor bedrooms," Colin said, surprised Barry had not mentioned them.

"They've been done away with now. Too risky. There were three, made out of a big Victorian conservatory, converted. Three rooms and a bathroom."

"Go on, please."

"It was while he was there, in the middle of a Saturday night. His was the only one of the three garden rooms, as we called them, where the thieves could have entered."

"Why?"

"The other two had shutters which the tenants used. Fred never used his shutters. Said he would suffocate."

"I suppose he said he didn't hear the burglars. But he must have, if they came through his room."

"He was not in his room. He was in mine."

A real alibi and no alibi. The most useful kind. Cast-iron alibis, if fake, can be broken. Indiarubber ones, like this, can bend but jump back into their former shape. Jim *could* have left his room, empty, vulnerable, on purpose to admit his friends. They had taken out a pane of glass and left it out. The big windows creaked when they were pushed up or down and the partitions between the garden rooms were not sound-proof. It was Jim who had raised the alarm, at four in the morning.

But who could prove his collaboration? He had been with Mrs Woodford-Smyth since eleven the night before. The night porter had been gagged and bound at his desk in the hall at twelve-thirty a.m.; set upon out of the shadows by four masked, silent-footed men as he sat under a single light, reading and dozing.

"Fred went to his room down the back staircase and found his window broken and gaping, so he said, as soon as he opened the door. He ran along to the hall at once and found the porter. He untied him and called the police, himself."

"So you had to confirm his story?" Colin said thoughtfully. Much was now clear concerning this case. Jim's methods, his callous indifference towards his victims, again revolted him.

"I refused at first." Mrs Woodford-Smyth's voice had grown harsher as this part of her story emerged. "He said if I wouldn't support him and tell the truth he would drag me into it. Suggest *I* had seduced *him* when he was hard up. Suggest I had lured him to my room so that the thieves could get in without disturbing anyone. That was when I first realised he was a criminal. Only the man who really *had* let them in would have invented such a lie."

"Did you tell all this to the police?"

"No. It was too dreadful. The whole thing. His behaviour— his treachery—the shock. It made me ill. My doctor sent me into hospital. My solicitor advised me to say as little as possible. The police didn't need me in the end, thank God. They explained their suspicions of Fred, as I told you, but it came to nothing. They had caught one of the thieves. Not the most important, but they got a conviction and that had to satisfy them, it seems. It was a near thing for me and of course, though I wasn't named at the trial of that man, all my friends knew who was meant. Friends, indeed! I soon learned I had none."

Colin could offer her no comfort. He kept silent until she spoke again, which she did very soon.

"It was rather a miracle the police were able to trace one of the culprits at all—the thieves, I mean. Only one set of fingerprints. They must have worn gloves, but this man had taken his off to light a cigarette. So they said. Yes, I know it sounds absurd, but it came out at the trial. The fingerprints were on a table where there was an ashtray with a box of matches. He'd used this box and touched the table before putting on his gloves again."

"Crazy!" Colin said. "Hadn't they a lighter between them?"

"Apparently not. The policeman who interviewed me said criminals always made silly mistakes. He was right. Fred had already made several."

At last, Colin thought, at last we've got there. The case against Fred Holmes.

It was quite a simple affair, just as obvious, just as flagrant as his former impudent conspiracy. Fred Holmes had no job, his business claims were lies, his need for financial support purely personal. He had fleeced Mrs Woodford-Smyth of several thousand pounds, more than half her small capital. He had paid her back a few sums in so-called dividends at the high rate of interest he had promised her. But the money was not earned by any form of investment, it was merely part of the capital he had stolen from her.

In addition to this continuing fraud, which had lasted for

H

the best part of a year, he had used her cheque book, forging
her signature with the same skill, the same reckless contempt
for risk he had shown as Ivan Totteridge. With, naturally, the
same result, when Mrs Woodford-Smyth, at last rebelling
against her servitude, her painful, ridiculous infatuation, had
made some private inquiries, assisted by her bank manager
and had gone to the police on her own account.

Fred Holmes, convicted without very much trouble, was put
away for two years.

"Wasn't that rather lenient?" Colin said, remembering the
former trial and the court-martial. "I mean, it was less than
the time before."

Mrs Woodford-Smyth's voice trembled with fury as she
answered.

"Lenient? It was disgraceful! Disgusting! D'you know
what the jury said? Guilty, but recommended for mercy,
because he had been encouraged to form this association
by the very person who had accused him. Meaning me, of
course."

"That was his defence, I suppose?" Colin suggested.

"His only defence. No dishonesty, he said. Just payment for
services rendered. Services! —" she broke down, sobbing wildly,
scrabbling in her bag for a handkerchief to stop the tears from
ruining her make-up.

It was not such a bad defence, either, Colin decided, if you
didn't mind presenting yourself as an unscrupulous gigolo. No
crime, nothing illegal in that profession. Prices, as in all forms
of honest prostitution, satisfaction given, were decided between the parties concerned. In a way she had only got what
she deserved, even if she hadn't bargained for it. The jury's
attitude was understandable. Except for the forgeries. Bloody
silly clot to fall for that again.

Mrs Woodford-Smyth took some time to recover. To assist
in this and complete his inquiries into her case Colin
approached the subject of the diary, its contents, the question
of the blood group.

"Blood group?" asked Mrs Woodford-Smyth vaguely. "What's that?"

But it was noticeable that her tears stopped very abruptly, that she turned to look at Colin for the first time, that her little eyes, though red-rimmed, with puffy eyelids, were focussed sharply upon him.

"Did he never tell you? He was always very anxious about himself, I believe."

"Oh, that! Scared of road accidents. Yes, he certainly was. But he said he carried a safety precaution with him."

"Didn't he tell you what that was?"

"He showed me. More than once. In a little old diary. A set of letters."

"His blood group."

"Oh, was that what it was?"

"Surely you knew. He must have told you if he showed it to you."

"I have very little knowledge of medical matters, Dr Frost."

But the sharpness in the little eyes had grown as she spoke, reflecting the hatred that had conquered and dispersed her former silly love.

Colin recoiled from it. He wanted nothing more, now, than to drive this horrible old creature back to her dreary lodging.

Mrs Woodford-Smyth saw she had not improved her own image by her frankness. She was used to this. It was part of the bitterness of age and the impertinent candour of modern youth. So she asked, with dignity, to be taken home. Arrived there, she expressed dignified thanks for a most enjoyable meeting and an excellent lunch. She did not say she hoped they might meet again; it was too unlikely; moreover, highly undesirable. Already he was cast for the villain's part in this little piece of fresh humiliation.

Three women who hated the dead man's guts, Colin thought as he drove off. Three? Surely four? The missing

Clarice Field. The most likely of the lot, because the last in point of time. Present, too, at the accident. Well, Barry would have to cope with that angle, if he was still keen.

When they met again later that day, to drive back to Brackenfield, Colin put this to the journalist. Discussing Clarice helped both of them to get the taste of Mrs Woodford-Smyth out of their mouths. And Barry was still keen.

CHAPTER TWELVE

In the meantime Inspector Rawlinson had not been idle. Hearing nothing of Colin's activities with the Press, he decided that the young registrar had given up his independent inquiries after the warning he had been given. This was gratifying to Inspector Rawlinson. He continued his search for details of Alec Hilton's stay in Brackenfield.

The man had worked reasonably well on the demolition site, though no one had taken much notice of him. The foreman of his particular gang remembered him and agreed that he had a skilled approach to his job. He had made several suggestions to do with breaking up the building they were on. As these involved the use of high explosive they were turned down by the management. But the foreman had been quite impressed.

Rawlinson was also impressed, by the man's audacity in making such a barefaced attempt to get hold of a commodity he used in his real trade, for Hilton was an expert safe-breaker. The inspector did not give this fact to the foreman, but he reported the latter's words to his colleagues at Scotland Yard, where they caused some amusement. Apart from this it did seem likely that Hilton was in Brackenfield chiefly to watch Jim Sparks. Which he was able to do without direct contact, through the club hostess, Clarice Field.

The girl was still missing when Rawlinson completed his

notes on Alec Hilton. He thought he had reached another dead end. But a few days later, in fact the day after Colin and the journalist had entertained Mrs Woodford-Smyth, a message came through from London. Clarice Field had been sighted in a pub in Wandsworth. She had not been traced to her present lodgings yet. She had been seen with another woman, who appeared to be a total stranger to her, not a friend. A close watch would be kept in the neighbourhood and further reports might be expected.

Rawlinson considered going to London, but after some thought decided he could do very little good there. For one thing he had never met Clarice Field. He had a police photograph of her which would not be very helpful. A girl could change her whole appearance with her hair style. If you knew her voice and mannerisms this would not deceive you, but it would be effective if you had only her description. He needed to know a great deal more about her before he took any part in the hunt. Even if his superiors would allow him to go. Enthusiasm for this particular case had not grown in Brackenfield. It would never do to plunge in and fail.

The next best move, the inspector finally decided, was to see the club manager again, tell him Clarice was in London, observe his reactions.

He went to the club that evening, but the manager was not there.

"Mr Gregson is in London," a smooth young man in a dinner jacket told him. "Can I help you?"

He was not at all disconcerted when he learned his questioner's name and profession.

"Well, well," he said cheerfully. "Would you care to come into the office? If there's anything I can do—"

Rawlinson followed him into a small room, sparsely furnished, with a table, a few chairs, typewriter and a filing cabinet.

"This is not Mr Gregson's office," said the inspector, looking round. The manager's office, where he had been on one occasion soon after the accident, had been larger and most comfortably upholstered.

"Oh no. This is mine. Assistant manager."

"I have not seen you before, Mr—?"

"Trueman. Bob Trueman."

"I was hoping to see Mr Gregson in connection with a Miss Field who was employed here for about a year up to six weeks ago."

"Clary? Yes, I know her."

"Know her or knew her?"

"I don't quite get—"

"When did you last see Miss Field?"

"I've known her off and on for years."

"That isn't what I asked you. When did you last see her?"

Mr Trueman looked surprised. He gave the impression, perhaps he simply wanted to give the impression, that he was not used to this sort of needling. He remained silent.

"Put it another way," Rawlinson said quietly. "How long have you been working here?"

"Three weeks."

"So you did not meet Miss Field at this club. You knew her before you came here?"

"Obviously. I said so just now."

"Then perhaps you will tell me when that was and where you met?"

The young man frowned, then laughed.

"In London. Years ago. Satisfied?"

"Whereabouts in London?"

"Does it matter where?"

"Perhaps so. Perhaps not." The inspector paused, then said carelessly. "She's back in London now, of course."

Mr Trueman's face changed remarkably.

"You're kidding! The old bastard! He's known all this time. I'll—"

"Hold it, Trueman! Are you referring to Gregson?"

"Stop kidding! As if you didn't know! Clary in town. Me

stuck here in this joint! By God, the damned, double-cross-ing—!"

He was out of his chair and had reached the door before Rawlinson, standing up, said, "Where are you going? Don't be a fool, Trueman. Come back and tell me what's been going on between you and Gregson. Or rather, not been going on. Been taking advantage of you, has he? Leaving you in charge here while he slips off. How often? Since you've been here, I mean?"

The young man left the door and returned slowly to the table. Both men sat down again.

"Now," Rawlinson said quietly, "forget Gregson for the moment. Go back to Miss Field. Tell me about her. How long exactly have you known her?"

"Years, I told you. Since we were both kids. I've been in clubs since I left school. So's she."

"How old are you, Mr Trueman?"

"Twenty-three. What's that got to do with it?"

The inspector ignored the question.

"So you knew Miss Field at the time she formed an associa-tion with—Fred Holmes, he called himself, then."

"Here, wait a bit! That's not right. It was the other chap, the big bruiser. Treated her like dirt, too."

"Describe this man. No, take a look at this."

Inspector Rawlinson pulled out of his pocket the Yard photograph of Alec Hilton. Trueman responded immediately.

"That's him. The dicks after him, are they?" A thought seemed to strike him. "This car inquest here, everyone's in-terested in. Fellow stuck in the back. Was that Hilton's work?"

"Well, was it?"

"I'm asking you. I never saw him around in Brackenfield."

"He left more than three weeks ago. Miss Field saw him, though. One of your other girls did, too. You never heard that?"

"Certainly not!" Bob Trueman's smooth cheek had grown pale. "I swear it! You've got to believe me!"

"If you are such a friend of Miss Field's I'd have thought she'd tell you."

"She never! She was too stuck on that Jim Sparks or Fred Holmes or whatever his bloody name was to be telling me anything important."

Inspector Rawlinson found this confusing. The girl seemed to switch her attentions back and forth too readily.

"Let's get this straight," he said heavily. "Miss Field had an association with Alec Hilton. How long ago did it start? Can you tell me that?"

"Five or six years. That's only a guess, mind you. I wasn't in contact with her all the time."

"When were you sure of the association?"

"Couple of years back. She was living with the bastard, then."

"Later she was interested in Sparks as Holmes. At her trial she was charged with harbouring and receiving, but was convicted on the first charge only. She was in a job at the time, swore she'd taken none of the money, he hadn't offered her any, only paid for his keep. But he was living with her for several months before we caught up with him."

Bob Trueman's lip curled at that 'we'. This country copper thought he was Scotland Yard, now, did he? Slowly and insolently he helped himself to a cigarette from an open packet on his desk, then pushed the packet towards the inspector. Rawlinson ignored it, looked the young man very straight in the eye and went on.

"Now. She serves her time, full remission, comes out, her old job won't have her, Gregson down here takes her on. You've followed her career. You get taken on by Gregson, too."

"Not then. I lost track of her. By the time I caught up, she'd been here quite some time and she'd got the job at the bar for Jim."

"How did you feel about that?"

"Feel about it? I'm not with you. What was I supposed to feel?"

"Hadn't Jim taken the girl? Didn't that mean anything to you personally?"

Trueman's eyes narrowed.

"Haven't I made it clear," he said softly, "that Clary was Alec's girl? For keeps, if he wanted it that way. She let Jim hide in her flat while the heat was on, but that was an order, see? An order from Alec." His voice rose as he went on speaking. "An order. Like writing to him after she came out. Getting him fixed up here. Getting Greg to take him. Orders. Or else!"

The hand with the cigarette was shaking now. Inspector Rawlinson watched it for a few seconds, then got up to go.

"Thank you for your co-operation," he said. "There's only one more question I'd like to ask. Is it true that you were genuine surprised just now to hear that Miss Field is in London?"

Bob Trueman opened the door of his office without answering, led the way to the open door of the club and stood aside for the inspector to pass out.

"You've made up your own mind, haven't you?" he said. "Whatever I told you wouldn't alter it."

"That's probably true," the inspector said cheerfully. "So long, Trueman. I'd keep away from London at present, if I were you. Probably not for long, now."

"And you can keep away from her, damn you!" Bob muttered at the retreating figure. Then he went back to the noisy hall, the bouncing figures, the blaring band, the silent, entwined couples in the shadows.

Back at the police station, Rawlinson got in touch with Scotland Yard. He reported his interview with Bob Trueman.

"I don't know if you have anything on this lad," he said. "I think it's unlikely, but he knows more about the Hilton set-up than is good for him, if Alec Hilton is all you say. I don't think he realised how much he did leak to me. At this end Gregson needs watching. He's making regular visits to London, just now. Perhaps to see Field."

This news was welcome at the Yard. A plan of action was worked out and agreed. Rawlinson's man, watching the club, reported Gregson's return late that night, after the public rooms were closed. The club manager let himself in at a side door. No lights appeared in the front of the building.

This was not surprising. The inspector knew that Gregson lived with his wife and a schoolboy son in a flat at the back on the first floor. Another man, patrolling the rear of the building, reported lights on in the flat all evening. These were put out soon after Gregson's return.

For nearly two weeks neither the club manager nor his assistant left Brackenfield for London, either by car or train. Rawlinson kept a watch both on the club and the railway station.

Since Gregson's car had been written off by his insurance company as a total wreck he had not attempted to buy another, perhaps in some wild hope that he might get compensation from the dead man's estate, perhaps in order to avoid any further local publicity. In any case he had travelled to London by rail, becoming familiar to the ticket collector and porters as a new regular commutor, though they did not know who he was. They were able, at a later date, to confirm his many appearances on the platform both going and coming back.

On Saturday afternoon, ten days after Rawlinson had seen Bob Trueman at the club, the expected happened. Two messages arrived for the inspector within a few minutes of one another. Gregson had left the club in a taxi, followed after fifteen minutes by Trueman in his own car. Gregson had arrived at the railway station and caught the three-fifteen p.m. express to London. Trueman had not been seen at the station at all.

Rawlinson immediately got in touch with his opposite number at the Yard, who arranged to meet him ten minutes after opening time at the pub in Wandsworth recently frequented by Clarice Field. Then Rawlinson, with a detective-sergeant driving, set off for London as well.

The journey was uneventful, the pub easily found. Having located it Rawlinson drove to the nearest police station, where he left the car and the driver, after explaining his mission to the superintendent there. Alone, he decided, he would not be noticed as anything but a stranger. But together with his sergeant, of similar build and dress, the doubtful characters, the informers, any other hangers-on of the underworld, would be likely to spot their calling.

At the given time Rawlinson pushed open the half-glazed inner door of the saloon bar, found it empty and turned into the public bar. There he saw his colleague and after collecting a pint of bitter joined him with the nod of a casual acquaintance.

This room was very much larger than the unpopular saloon, very full of people and already hazy with tobacco smoke. Rawlinson sat down with his back to the bar, facing his companion.

"We're not all here yet," the Yard man said. "That is, the girl's in the corner on your right, tucked in against the wall with two men opposite her. I haven't identified either, but they're not your fat chap, nor the one we're both after."

Rawlinson took a leisurely glance round, then moved again to keep his face from the company.

"Gregson's at the bar now," he said. "Short chap, light overcoat, balding."

"I've got him. He doesn't know me, of course. He's been looking in our direction, though. Ah, now he's seen Field. He's edging their way. Not sure who she's with, I suppose. Still no sign of Hilton," he added, in a voice so low Rawlinson could only guess the name.

Very cautiously, his mug held up to his face as if drinking from it, he moved his head from side to side. Certainly Gregson was there, leaning against the bar now, obviously trying to attract the girl's attention. And beyond Gregson, speaking to the barmaid, was Bob Trueman, his black hair as sleek as ever, his eyes fixed on the mirror behind the bar, in which no doubt he, too, could watch Miss Field. Who was leaning forward now, careless of anyone else around her, speaking urgently, hurriedly, fearfully, to the two men whose backs never moved, whose drinks stayed untouched on the table beside them.

CHAPTER THIRTEEN

Barry Summers had not been far behind the police in discovering Clarice Field. This he did by the simple process of following Amos Gregson on one of the club manager's expeditions to London.

By this time Barry's editor was solidly behind him in his investigations. The whole story was coming nearer to Brackenfield, even if its roots were in London. Barry was able to go off as he wished without wasting time getting permission. So, having noticed taxis drawing up fairly often outside the club and having then waited to confirm, as he guessed, that the carless Gregson used them, he followed to the station twice, then went to the station on the next occasion in time to catch the train himself.

He lost Gregson in London the first time, though his own taxi managed to stick on the other's tail until it disappeared down a side road while Barry's was held up at some traffic lights. So he got out, paid it off and did a reconnaissance on foot, noting the pubs, their names and the names of the streets. On his way home in the train he made quite a good map of the district, which he afterwards compared with a large scale printed one.

It was a week before he picked up Gregson again on a London train. This time he kept close behind him as he hurried to the taxi rank, and pretending to misunderstand the manager's action, made as if to open the door while overhearing the address Gregson gave. It was one of the roads on his map. Gregson was in the second pub he tried. He was alone.

Barry stayed at the bar, watching. As soon as the girl came in he recognised her. He had been afraid of this. He had visited the club in Brackenfield a few times more often than Colin had, but mostly before Clarice started work there. All the same, he decided that if he knew who she was the moment she entered this place, the chances were she would recognise him, at least know that he came from Brackenfield and on that account might be dangerous.

But Clarice was far too intent upon the men and women sitting at the tables or on the benches that ran round two of the walls, to notice anyone at the bar. So Barry risked continuing to watch. He saw her go up to Gregson, saw him greet her and get up to fetch her a drink. Barry emptied his glass, slipped away from the bar before Gregson arrived there and without looking round went quickly out into the street. He then decided he had done enough for one day and went home. He had definite news to report, both to his editor and to Colin.

But it was not until the latter's next free weekend that Barry returned to London, this time bringing the registrar with him. It was on this same Saturday that Amos Gregson had gone up again from Brackenfield, followed discreetly on the road by Inspector Rawlinson. The two backs that the inspector had not recognised in the pub belonged to Barry Summers and Colin Frost.

Miss Field was not at all pleased to see them, but she was, as usual, under orders. So she decided to let events take their course, without making any personal effort to alter them. In fact, for the first time since the car smash, the spirit of rebellion was stirring in her. The sight of two young men, whose company she had enjoyed on the rare occasions she had met them, increased the stirring. A few glasses of the vodka that was now

her favourite tipple brought it bubbling to the surface. But for
a time she was suspicious and careful.

"Not got the dicks in your pockets, have you?" she asked,
when the small talk faltered.

"Of course not." Colin was indignant. "We just want to
know exactly what happened that night you and Sparks
pinched the Hillman."

"Now look here—" she began, her hands on the table, half
rising from her seat.

Colin laid his own hands over hers. She stared at him, sank
back and when he released her said, nodding at Barry, "Wants
it for the *Mercury*, eh?"

"Partly that," Barry agreed. "But only when it won't do you
any harm, Clary. I swear it. Mostly it's because of what Colin's
interested in. Tell her," he said to Colin. "Tell her about the
other doctor."

So Colin repeated his defence of Patel, his determination to
exonerate the Indian's impulsive mistake.

Miss Field listened, sympathised, looked puzzled. As the
other women had done, Colin reminded himself.

"I expect you knew about this blood group complex of
Jim's?" he asked her.

"Come again."

"Complex. Obsession. Had it on his mind a lot. Told people
about it. Told you, I'm sure."

"Oh, yeah," she said. "Yeah. I knew he was frightened of
accidents."

"More than that. Didn't he tell you about blood trans-
fusions? That he'd got his blood group marked down."

"I don't remember."

"Did he never show it you, written down in a little book? A
little old diary?"

Comprehension dawned at last.

"That! Why didn't you say before? Of course we all knew
that little book. Was that what it was for?"

He wasn't going to get any further with her, Colin decided.

It might be she was as stupid as she made herself out, perhaps it was only a pose, a studied pose. Impossible to know.

"If he was frightened of accidents," Barry cut in, "why did he get into one? Driving too fast? Scared he wouldn't get away with a stolen car?"

"You can say that again."

She emptied her glass in one gulp. All the restraints of the last weeks, of the years before them, broke as the memory of that hideous night poured over her.

"We were leaving," she said defiantly. "We were leaving the club and that silly old town and fat Greg, always pawing at you, enough to make you throw up. We were leaving."

"You and Jim?" asked Barry cautiously.

"What d'you think, for heaven's sake? When Alec—"

She covered her mouth suddenly, with both hands, terrified.

"It's all *right*," Colin soothed. "We know about him. At least we know a bit. Don't we, Barry?"

"Yes," the journalist agreed stoutly, thoroughly mystified. "Yes, of course."

"Let's get it straight," Colin urged. "You wanted to quit. You and Jim. Where were you going?"

"Ireland. Then the States if we could get enough poppy. You see, they'd dropped Jim when he was nicked. No good to them any more. So when I went and got this job in Brackenfield and then got Jim there as soon as he was out, they started in, see."

"This Alec did, you mean?"

"Well, they were sort of connected with the club. Alec was boss, as usual." She was speaking the name quietly now, perhaps because Barry had brought her yet another vodka. "We thought, at least it was Jim's idea, if we went in old Greg's car we could get a start without anyone at the club thinking anything. Greg had lent Jim his car every now and then. Sent him errands in it. So we thought it wouldn't be noticed. Just before opening time, everyone busy. You know."

"I can imagine," Colin said. "What went wrong?"

"That devil must have guessed and warned him. Jim did put our suitcases in the boot a bit earlier. He said no one saw him. He must have been wrong."

"So?"

"We left very quickly at the end. Just went out, not speaking, got into the car and Jim drove off. Not hurrying, all quite quiet, till we were clear of the town."

"But the alarm was given to the police almost at once. How did that happen?"

She shook her head.

"I told you. Greg must have been tipped off. Must have been two of them on to it."

"Was it this Alec?"

"No. Someone else. Alec was with us. In the car."

She stared beyond them, shuddered as the memory of that bitter shock came back to her, then her head drooped and her hand went out again to her glass.

"He was in the car!" Barry was astonished. He had met this situation in fiction but had never believed it could really be managed.

"That's right. On the floor at the back. It was dark when we went into the yard at the club. We'd arranged not to speak, not a word. Just climb in and we'd be off in a jiffy. Jim had it all timed and it worked. I never looked at anything but the back door of the club to see no one had spotted us and Jim only looked at the car panel to put in the key and then ahead at the open gate. He didn't put the lights on till we were out in the road. It only took seconds, the whole start."

"I believe you," said Barry doubtfully, but he still wondered. Clary belonged to a criminal gang, living a lie with thieves and liars. Why should he believe her now?

But Colin urged her on.

"Don't stop there!" he said, with excitement in his voice. "You can't stop now. This chap was in the car at the back. When did he pop up? After the smash or before?"

"Before." Her eyes, fixed on his, darkened as the terror of

that moment came back to her. "He told Jim to go back. He had a knife."

"Ah." For Colin this meant the first step in Patty's final justification. "He threatened Jim with it, did he?"

"He—" She hesitated, paused, but went on firmly. "Yes. Threatened him. At least—"

There was again doubt in her eyes, doubt and fear. Barry saw it, interpreting the situation his own way, based on his experience of so many like situations.

"Miss Field," he said, taking her attention away from Colin, "was this man, Alec, whoever he is—was he jealous of Sparks? In relation to you, I mean?"

She laughed, suddenly, harshly.

"Boy, are you green!" she told him.

"You said he menaced you both with his knife. Did you really mean that?"

"Of course I meant it."

"But Jim didn't stop, did he? He had no intention of stopping, turning, going back?"

She shivered. She said, this time in almost a whisper, "He didn't have time."

Barry and Colin exchanged glances. They were nearly home. Both of them now believed what the girl was trying to tell them. That the gangster Alec, furious with Jim both for taking his girl and very nearly escaping with her, had plunged the knife into his rival, reckless of the result to all three of them.

Colin repeated, "He didn't have time. For what, Miss Field? To miss being stabbed? Or to get round that bend? Or both? How was it? Tell us. You must tell us!"

But while he was speaking both he and Barry, intent upon her every expression, had seen a change come over her face. Her eyes widened, fear flooding into them, her mouth grew rigid, half open. She was looking past them at the door of the pub. It was partly open. In the shadow between it and the outer door there was a darker shadow, the figure of a man.

I

Miss Field got slowly to her feet. Barry and Colin pushed back their chairs.

"Now what's the matter?" Colin asked. "You must be able to tell us how the smash happened. You can't stop now."

She gave a loud, unnatural laugh.

"I can't stop now? No, I can't stop! Not here with you two going on at me. I won't stop! Let me out. Let me out, damn you!"

She was struggling to move the table between them so that she could leave her corner. Barry held the table firm.

"You can go when you've answered my question," he told her, ignoring the faces that were turning in their direction, and a movement that was taking place on the other side of the room. It was too maddening to be baulked of the truth when he was nearly there, his story so very nearly complete. "Come on, Clary. Be a sport. What made Sparks drive into that coach? How did he get the knife in his ribs? You *do* know! You *must* know!"

Barry, so intent upon the girl, had not seen the figure in the doorway. But Colin had. He followed the direction of Clarice's fixed gaze, had seen a movement—was it a hand signal—and guessed the reason. The girl was being summoned to break off her conversation. She dared not disobey.

As he swung round again Colin saw at the bar a man he thought he recognised. A neat figure standing there, a glass in his hand, leaning back, his eyes upon Clarice, who had now squeezed out of her corner and was standing quite still, white-faced, uncertain. She too, had seen Bob Trueman.

Colin jumped up, Barry was already standing. More heads were turning now, curious to see what was going to happen. A girl and two men, a tense quarrel, though they were all quiet enough.

Barry would not give up. He laid a hand on the girl's arm, repeating his questions in the same words.

She shook him off. Her face flushed, the frozen look breaking now into anger.

"It was an accident!" she said loudly, too loudly. "Damn you both, an accident! Let me alone. *Let me alone!*"

She was gone before they could move to stop her. They saw her dodging between the tables and the customers to reach the door. They saw an arm come out to secure her as the inner door swung open. They saw, through its glass, the lights of the street shine out as the outer door opened, then fade as both doors swung back.

Two men had started after Clarice as she crossed the room. They nearly jammed in the doors, but both were agile.

"Who—?" said Colin quickly, turning to Barry.

"The young one? Bob Trueman, assistant manager at the club."

"I thought I'd seen his face somewhere. Knows her, I suppose?"

"Known her for years. Told me so."

"Who was outside? She was scared cold."

Barry shook his head. It was easy, too easy, to guess. Pointless to speculate.

"What next?" he said, feeling deflated, helpless.

"What *next*?" a furious voice said behind them. "What *more*? Haven't I warned you not to get under my feet? What the devil d'you think you're doing here, anyway?"

It was Inspector Rawlinson, furious and frustrated. Behind him, looking very miserable indeed, stood Amos Gregson.

CHAPTER FOURTEEN

The two young men were speechless, taken aback a second time by action too swift to follow.

"Outside!" Rawlinson ordered and turning, repeated to the unwilling Gregson, "You, too. Outside!"

In the street Colin realised the full extent of his and Barry's intervention. No sooner had Rawlinson stepped on to the pavement than a black police car glided to a stop at the kerb and the driver jumped out.

"Get in!" Rawlinson barked. Colin first, followed by Barry, and then the club manager, piled into the back of the car. A uniformed officer, appearing from beside the pub, checked a tendency on Gregson's part to hang back. The doors slammed, the car started.

"Move into the middle, Gregson," the inspector said from his seat beside the driver, and when Gregson obediently squeezed between Colin and Barry, squashing them against the sides of the car, added, "I hold you two responsible for seeing he doesn't get away when we stop at the lights."

Colin felt like laughing. A picture of fat Gregson stumbling to the side of the road through a jam of waiting cars and panting away down a side street made a pleasantly ludicrous picture. But he kept a straight face, nodded obediently, locked the door beside him and motioned Barry to do likewise.

For a little while Rawlinson was busy on the radio, both reporting to Scotland Yard and taking messages. It seemed to the listening men in the back, trying to interpret a few connected sentences, that quite a large operation was in being. This journey was clearly no free drive to Scotland Yard or any other police centre. They were part of a hunt, the hunt for Clarice Field.

"So now you know." Inspector Rawlinson said, turning round to look at the three behind him. "You needn't pretend ignorance. You've each had a hand in obstructing and if I find you've wrecked this operation you're for it, me lads."

"I haven't done a thing," Gregson protested. "You've no possible right—"

"You went to meet Miss Field," Rawlinson said. It was a statement, not a question.

"Why not? You've nothing against her—or me—even if you had, it's still a free country, isn't it? Until you're charged."

"You knew where to find her. Only a week ago you were still denying any knowledge of her whereabouts."

"I don't know where she lives. I swear it."

"Possibly. But you knew where to find her, didn't you? You never told me that."

"You didn't ask me. Anyway, you knew, yourself, she was going to that pub. A week ago, you knew. Why should I tell you something you already knew?"

"How do you know I knew already?"

"I saw you there."

One up to old Amos, Colin thought. The inspector saw the quick pleased grin and resented it.

"What were *you* doing there, Dr Frost?"

"Interviewing Miss Field, Inspector. Barry here found out she used that pub."

"Bob Trueman confirmed it," Barry added.

The inspector broke off to take another message, at the end of which he and his driver had a brief conference in low voices. Though the three in the back of the car leaned forward as far as they dared, they heard only a word or two. It seemed, though, that some confusion had developed. The chase was not going as planned.

"Don't you want to know what Miss Field said to us about the accident?" Colin ventured.

The broad back in front of him did not move.

"She and Jim Sparks had decided to quit," Barry joined in. "They took Mr Gregson's car so they could get away quickly without anyone suspecting they were not on some errand for him."

"But the other man was hiding in the car," Colin took up the story. "He tried to make Sparks turn round and go back. He threatened him with a knife."

Still there was no response from the front passenger seat, though Gregson had begun to make protesting noises, only controlled by Barry's jabbing elbow.

"She was going to tell us some more," Barry said. "But she

saw whoever it was at the door and that put the lid on her.
Just before she left she said it was all an accident. Meaning the
stab wound and the crash, I think."

"I think she meant the stabbing," Colin argued. "And
I think that was a lie because she was afraid to speak the
truth."

"You do, do you?" said Inspector Rawlinson. He turned
slowly now to look at his passengers. "And what the hell use is
all that to me? I've a good mind to charge you two with
obstruction here and now, only I happen to be busy."

And far away from anywhere, Colin thought. Streets and
houses had thinned out, shops vanished. They were still
whistling along at a very good speed, on a main road, bordered
by houses with gardens. He had not the faintest idea where
they were, but since they had not crossed the river concluded
they were somewhere in Kent or Surrey, and south or west of
the Croydon bulge.

The police driver interrupted to ask a question. Inspector
Rawlinson got back on the intercom. This time he made no
coherent answers, merely accepted orders. At the end of it he
stopped the car in the next lay-by and after a few more
exchanges told the driver to go back to Wandsworth. In total
silence and at a much reduced speed the police and their unwilling passengers drove away again.

In spite of the slower going it took less time than on the
outward journey. Colin concluded that they must have been
engaged in a genuine chase involving a certain amount of
dodging moves on the part of the quarry. From the back seat
he had not been able to identify any particular car they had
been following. In daylight there would have been some
chance of doing so; at night it was impossible.

The silence continued until they were back in London and
nearing the pub. Then the inspector said, "You drove up, I
suppose? Not you, Gregson. I know you used the railway.
Where did you park your car, Dr Frost?"

Colin told him. He and Barry were turned out at the parking spot, with a final word of warning. Inspector Rawlinson transferred himself to the back of the police car. Before Colin had unlocked his door, the Law had gone.

"Where's he off to now?" Colin said, as he started his own engine.

"Back home, I'd guess," Barry answered with a yawn. "God, I'm whacked. The criminal life is not for me. I must tell that to my editor."

"If we'd really been in on it, it might have been quite fun," Colin said wistfully. "As luggage, under threat, it was all a bit of a bore. But I'd certainly like to know why they called it off."

"I'd like to know what happened to Bob Trueman," Barry said.

"I'm damned hungry," Colin answered.

They stopped at an all night coffee shop before they left Wandsworth. A couple of hot dogs and mugs of a hot but tasteless fluid gave them some comfort. By the time they reached Brackenfield they had decided that the evening had not been a total failure. On the other hand Colin was no nearer to solving his real problem. Barry agreed.

"I'll keep in touch," he said. "You think it over and if you get any ideas let me know. But nothing spectacular. Rawlinson means business and we've both got our jobs to think of."

"Yes, uncle," Colin answered, laughing. But he knew the position was serious. Anything he did now must on no account lead back to the police. Which seemed to be a contradiction in terms.

Meanwhile Inspector Rawlinson had a very profitable conversation with the club manager, who, frightened and dejected, decided that his only safe move was to put himself entirely at the disposal of the Law.

He had been the victim of a protection racket, managed by Alec Hilton and his associates. This had been going on ever since he had tried to escape them by transferring himself and his club to Brackenfield from his former premises in Chelsea.

Escape had, naturally, been impossible. Too many people knew him. Too many were afraid of Alec.

The persecution had not been very severe to begin with. Simply a percentage of the profits. Trouble began when he was told to engage Clarice Field, after her discharge from Holloway.

"I was pleased at first," Gregson said plaintively. "She was a good little hostess and a first-rate dancer. It was later when she got me to take on Jim Sparks. Told me he was in with Alec, which had been true, but wasn't any more. They'd ditched him on account of the boob he made over the last job he did for them. I'd no idea of this, naturally. Until Alec came down, blew his top and ordered me to get rid of him."

"Why didn't you?"

"Clary said if I did she'd leave herself. She said she was through with Alec. That wasn't true, either. Besides, there was Bob."

Gregson's little eyes gleamed viciously. He thought he understood now who had betrayed him to the police and how they had been able to plan the moves they had made that night. But he kept silent now. He had warned Rawlinson the club was in danger. He hoped he had transferred the protection to the right quarter. He need only carry on for a few months longer, through this winter, then he could sell out a going concern and retire on the proceeds added to his already substantial savings. It might not be easy. Clary had gone and Bob would have to go. He wished very much that he knew what had been the outcome of the chase that night and why it had been called off. At least as far as Rawlinson was concerned. Had Clary been secured or had she disappeared again? Where was she? And where was Bob?

Inspector Rawlinson, too, wished he knew the answers to these questions. Though he had a much clearer picture of the events of that night.

When Clarice Field had hurried out of the pub she was followed closely by Bob Trueman. It was he who pushed Alec from behind as the latter was pulling her towards his car, standing at the kerb, who snatched Clarice away and ran with her to his own sports car, parked a few yards further up the road.

All this was seen by the Yard detective, waiting outside the door of the pub and watching Hilton's movements. He too, had stepped forward to stop Miss Field's abduction, knowing that reinforcements were at hand in the police car that was at that moment drawing up in front of Hilton's car, between it and Trueman's.

For the next few seconds all was confusion on the pavement. The watching man went for Hilton; the new arrivals, seeing the girl running away, went for her and her companion. Bob and Clarice were too quick for them. They leaped into the sports car and were off with the police still ten yards behind. The latter dashed for their own car and gave chase.

Meanwhile, outside the pub, Hilton understood most of what was happening. The dicks were after him, he knew. But they also wanted Clary. He had lost her temporarily. How and to whom he had not had time to discover. But his own safety came first, as always. Finding himself alone with one man, the one who had closed with him, as he thought, freeing the girl to run off with another, he took a quick look round, then struggled violently, butting and jabbing with vicious energy. He was too much for his assailant, who reeled away from him. Jumping for his own car, now no longer obstructed by the police, he was able to get away before the Yard man had got back his breath and overcome the ringing in his head, before the arrival of a uniformed officer at the run.

The chase that followed consisted of four cars, Bob with Clarice in the lead, the London police following not far behind. Then Alec, who in spite of the risk was determined to find out where Clarice was going. Lastly Inspector Rawlinson in his Brackenfield police car.

It was not surprising that reinforcements were called in, patrols alerted, a few road blocks set up. The result was precisely nil. Alec Hilton, when his initial rage subsided, was far too wary, too experienced, to leave the shelter of the south London he knew so well. Besides, he was too late to effect anything useful. If the sports car was stopped, the pair in it arrested, he could not help them and only risked arrest himself. If they got away he could not follow through the cordon he knew would be in place by now.

So after a short run he slipped down a side turning, left the car he was in, which did not belong to him, and disappeared into a maze of side streets where presently he took another car and drove away to his home.

The police hunt continued for a time but Bob won, again chiefly because of the confusion at high levels. He was stopped at a road block, but the car was his own, which he could prove, licence and insurance were in order. Clarice said she was his wife. They were let through with no delay at all, much to the disgust of the first police car to reach the barrier. After this, warnings went out to towns and villages along the main road, but without much hope, for there were endless side turnings along which the fugitives could escape. It was not surprising that the direct hunt was called off and Inspector Rawlinson was told that nothing more could be done that night.

Amos Gregson returned to his club and paid no more visits to London. Indeed, he paid no visits at all outside his own premises, and bought an Alsatian to leave in the club rooms at night. He realised that he had broken the terms of his so-called protection and might receive some kind of unpleasant revenge in the near future. He did not feel he could rely altogether on the local police after he had ignored them for so long.

Bob Trueman did not reappear in Brackenfield, nor in any of his former London haunts. He had no criminal record, though he had been interviewed several times in connection with drug pushing at the clubs where he had worked. He had not been deeply involved on any of these occasions, nor had he ever supplied any really useful evidence. Playing a very

cool, very careful hand on the fringe of the game, Scotland
Yard thought. No one had bothered to investigate his early
life, his childhood story, even where he had lived before he got
his first job at a London club. Now that he had disappeared,
carrying off Clarice Field with him, they wished they had. If
the men at the road block had recognised him and had not
failed to get the number of his car correctly, they might not
have lost him. And lost Hilton, too. Very regrettable, indeed.

None of this concerned Inspector Rawlinson, except
indirectly. From Colin and Barry he had heard Miss Field's
story of the mad drive in the stolen Hillman. It confirmed
what he already knew; it did nothing to fill the important
detail of the sequence of events at the time of the crash. They
knew Alec Hilton had been in the car; they knew there had
been a knifing; they had the knife, with Jim Sparks's blood on
it. The girl had apparently insisted that it was an accident. Did
she mean the car smash was an accident, or the stabbing?
Until she was found and persuaded to speak, they could get no
further. There was a warrant out now for her arrest and for
Bob Trueman for aiding and abetting her. Inspector Rawlinson had no reason to think they would come his way, but
he continued to keep an eye on the club and the Gregson
family.

In London a rather different view prevailed. Clarice Field,
presumably still protected by Bob Trueman, might perhaps
act the part of the tethered goat in tempting that wild beast,
Alec Hilton, into the open. However, until they knew where
the bait was they could not lie in wait for the murderer. So the
hunt for the girl and her friend continued in widening circles
as the days passed. Without success.

Alec Hilton betrayed himself in the end. That he did not
escape, as hitherto he always had done, was due partly to luck,
largely to the swift intelligence of Police-Constable Sinclair, on
special duty at Brighton to guard pedestrians against their
normally suicidal tendencies at any seaside resort. After a
week of heavy storm there were gaps in the railings on the sea

wall, even in the pavement, at one spot in the roadway itself. The tide at the flood still cascaded over the wall.

Constable Sinclair was there among other extras lent by the inland county forces, to prevent accidents. His surroundings, seaward, were so formidable that he remained alert, moving slowly, watching carefully.

He saw a trio standing talking; apparently unaware that the rail beside them had gone. He walked towards them, prepared to order them to a safer place. The air was filled with the roar of the waves, wet with the falling spray from the last monster that had crashed on the wall. Intent upon their purpose the three did not notice his approach.

It was plain to Sinclair as he drew nearer that the talk had become a quarrel. A step or two more and he saw a knife flash. The girl flung herself backwards, fell into the gap and the next great wave thundered down on her.

Constable Sinclair did not hesitate. He had seen as he passed it earlier the slope of rubble running down from the gap to the beach. The girl could not have fallen far, though the wave might have dragged her down to the shingle. He had also seen the second man leap through the gap after her. His job was to deal with crime. He brought the edge of his hand down on the attacker's arm; the knife dropped to the pavement. Sinclair flung both arms round the man, holding him close and yelling for reinforcements.

There were not many people about, it being early December and such a wild afternoon. But those who had come out were hardy natives of the town, not gawping visitors. They understood the hazards of winter by the sea and came running.

"Girl down there," panted Constable Sinclair. "Make a chain." And to a fisherman he recognised, "Give me a hand, Len. Chap tried to knife her."

Len secured the knife, which was lying near the feet of the swaying couple and as he straightened up, grinning, said hopefully, "Shall I give the bastard a jab or two?"

Alec gave a mighty heave at this, nearly breaking the constable's hold, but he found his own knife very near his throat, held in a steady hand. Len was not grinning now.

"Do that again and you get it right in the gizzard," he said. "Suicide while resisting arrest, eh, Tom?"

The prisoner stood very still, not defeated, just changing his tactics. When these fools were off their guard, he decided, he would break away, as he had so many times before in his aimless, violent life.

But he was out of luck. The less active, less strong helpers had called up others. A police patrol on a motorbike had arrived, had called up a police van and an ambulance. Alec was surrounded, secured, handcuffed, bundled into the van and driven away.

Meanwhile Bob Trueman, clinging with one hand to the broken rail halfway down the slope, had caught Clarice by her clothes with the other hand and held on while she pulled herself to her knees, struggling to move up to him.

The helpers above soon organised themselves in a cautious chain. Though as they came slowly down, pausing when a wave broke over them, the pebbles and lumps of brick and concrete showered down the slope on to Clarice, Bob managed to hold her until the rescuing hands seized her by both arms and half dragged, half carried her upwards. Bob followed close behind in case she slipped again.

Later that day, weak and exhausted, but otherwise un-harmed, Clarice was quite ready to talk. She understood her position fully at last. They had explained to her how she had compromised Bob Trueman.

"I had to," she said. "Alec wanted to kill me."

Inspector Rawlinson was there and his colleague from Scot-land Yard, together with two of the local CID. She was in a private ward of the hospital and in spite of what they had said to her she felt safe for the first time since she had stumbled out of the Hillman, five miles from Brackenfield.

"Alec tried to kill me in the car," she told the listening men. "He tried to make Jim go back, then when he wouldn't and I

said I wouldn't ever go back to him, he said he'd do me. I saw
he was mad enough, so I got down under the dashboard and
he leaned over the back of the seat, trying to get at me, but
Jim caught him by the wrist. It was awful! The car began to
sway about, but Jim held on, telling Alec to drop the knife and
we got to the bend and the car ran into the coach. Jim was still
holding Alec's wrist right up to the collision. When we struck I
think they both let go. The knife went into Jim by accident.
Alec was upside down over the front seat, he couldn't have
done it then. But it was me he meant it for. Same as he did
today."

"You actually saw the knife go into Sparks?"

She nodded, her face screwed up, remembering.

The men looked at one another. They had today's attempted
murder nicely buttoned up. This story would support it very
neatly. Alec was bound to get a nice big dollop of porridge.
Just what they'd wanted for a very long time.

Inspector Rawlinson said, "Miss Field, how did you get away
from Hilton immediately after the accident?"

"I'd bumped my head, but that was all. I was under the dashboard, as I said. I got a lot of bruises. I realised that later. At
the time I just scrambled out and ran away back along the
road, along the grass verge, I mean. I ran till I saw a telephone
box. Then I thought of Jim. Before that I thought they were
both dead, but I was afraid, just in case Alec wasn't. He must
have recovered almost at once."

"Why didn't you get help from the coach? And protection,
too?"

"And get picked up by all of you? And go back to Holloway
for nicking the car? No fear. I swore I'd never go there again.
I told Alec I'd never work for him again. Nor I will. I'd rather
die."

Looking round at the four stern faces she understood her
recent plight and began to cry bitterly, seeing no future now,
whatever way it went.

"Don't upset yourself," the Scotland Yard man said. "You've

given us some very valuable information. When you're feeling better we'll have another talk. After all, you're a valuable witness now. We've got to look after you. So don't be too downhearted."

Inspector Rawlinson said, "Would you like to see your friend, Mr Trueman? He saved your life today, you know. Like he did in Wandsworth not so long ago."

Clarice nodded. These dicks, so friendly, so darned dangerous, they knew it all. She hated their guts, but she couldn't help admiring them too, in a way. Poor Bob. Poor little brother, Bob. He was a good kid. She ought to have taken his advice and got out sooner. Yes, she'd like to thank Bob. Would they let him take her home again? For good?

CHAPTER FIFTEEN

News of Alec Hilton's dramatic arrest and the equally dramatic rescue of Clarice Field from death by stabbing or drowning came to Colin through the newspapers. The first accounts made good reading but gave no names. Colin would not have paid particular attention to them if Barry had not rung him up, in great excitement, the same evening, to explain who was concerned in these wild doings.

"Did you see they've nicked Alec Hilton?" he said. "Trying to do Clary on the sea front at Brighton? Or don't you have time to read the papers?"

"So that's who it was," Colin answered, equally excited. "Out in the open at last! Tell me more."

Barry described the scene as relayed to the *Brackenfield Mercury*.

"I'm going down to the magistrates' court tomorrow," he said. "Let you have all the gen when I get back."

"Fair enough," Colin answered and rang off. He was still coping with a very heavy day's work. The affair of the crooks, though interesting always and now apparently moving swiftly to some sort of conclusion, faded into the background. When he got to bed that night, after performing two emergency operations, he had quite forgotten them.

But the following evening, when Barry telephoned again, he was ready and anxious to learn what had happened in court that morning. He met Barry in the pub round the corner of the hospital.

"You talk," he said. "What's really been going on?"

"A hell of a lot," answered the journalist. "The main point that concerns you is that Clarice Field swears Hilton was mad with her for trying to run off with Sparks. She was really getting out, she says. They'd both decided to go straight."

"Loud laughter in court," said Colin.

"By no means. She sounded pretty convincing. Anyway, Hilton went for her in the car and was baulked by Sparks. He tried and failed to nab her in Wandsworth, had another go at her on the Brighton esplanade. If she hadn't had that gap behind her he'd have carved her up. As it was she fell and if it hadn't been for Bob Trueman she'd have been washed out to sea and drowned."

"Is Bob her new boy-friend? No, I mean old flame restored to favour?"

"Neither. He's her brother."

"*No!*"

"Sure thing. Three years younger, very devoted. Took up club work himself to keep an eye on her. Her real name is Mary Trueman. Show-biz name, Clarice Field."

"Well, well," said Colin. "Never a dull moment, is there? What happens next?"

"Hilton remanded in custody. Field remanded on bail."

"What for?"

"Failing to report to the police. It seems they let her out on licence from Holloway quite soon after she went in. They could still pull her back with something extra on account of Gregson's car."

"And Trueman?"

"Qualified pats on the back. The public considers him a hero. Risking his life for a girl who is only his sister. Marvellous example of old-fashioned family affection, moral values and so on. The local respectables have gone to town on it. Correspondence flooding in, I gather."

"Don't give me cheap cynicism. Can't you see we're back to square one. *Again.*"

"How so?"

Colin explained. If Hilton, in the car, brandishing his knife, intended it for Clarice, then the fact that on impact with the coach it plunged into Jim Sparks instead, surely must be pure accident. The attempted murder was in respect of Clarice, not Jim. The real attempt on Jim was not made by Hilton, but by whoever altered the blood group in the diary. And this succeeded, or contributed to the death, with the innocent but positive assistance of the unfortunate Ahmed Patel.

"I see what you mean," Barry said, nodding. "We need a lawyer's opinion on it, really, though. Hilton caused the accident, didn't he and the accident caused the death."

They went carefully over all the information they had collected so far concerning the life, habits, successes and failures of James Stowden, or Totteridge, Pearce, Holmes, Sparks.

"*Someone* altered that blood group," Colin said gloomily when the recital was over. "Some enemy had contact with him, sometime. We can knock out his wife. She knew the blood group and knew he had the right one when he left her house after his brief visit. She never saw him again."

"We've only got her word for both these statements."

"True enough. But I don't think she was lying. As for the other women, they were so vague— But I wouldn't say any of them was really capable. Except old Woodford-Smyth. She wanted revenge, all right. D'you think her tiny mind could work the blood group idea?"

"No," said Barry, with conviction. "And Clarice is out, because I believe her when she says she and Jim were quitting. *He* may not have meant it; I'll swear *she* did."

"He had an enemy," Colin insisted. "Somewhere along the line we've missed out on a vital clue. We know about a few women he cheated. There may be others. There may well be men. It was money he was after all the time. He stole from that firm he was in. He forged cheques."

"How about blackmail?" Barry suggested.

"That's right. How about blackmail?"

Colin got up to get another round of drinks at the bar. When he came back he said, "I've thought of something."

"Go ahead."

"When he was chucked out of the army, a friend of his was nearly chucked out, too. But he was a National Service chap, not a regular, so they let him finish his time. This is what Brigadier Stowden told me. I think we've got to find the chap. Uncle Will has a photo of the pair of them."

"Pair of who? Who's Uncle Will?"

"Sorry. The brigadier. Jim and his friend, Roy—Roy Waters. That's the name."

"I can't see what we get out of that."

"No? Suppose this Roy was really in the army fraud with Jim, though he managed to wriggle out—nearly. Suppose Jim met up with him years later. Nice subject for blackmail, don't you think?"

"*Did* they ever meet later?"

"I don't know. Uncle Will might. I do remember now he said, when he showed me the photograph of the two, both in uniform, he did say he himself never saw Roy again after the court-martial."

Barry stared.

"Is that *all* you remember?"

"No. He said he thought Roy was going in for medicine. My God, that's suggestive, isn't it? Why did I never go for that

before? If he qualified he'll be in the directory. Come on, we
can check that right away."

They went back to the medical school and to the library,
where they searched the current directory. But there was no
Roy Waters there.

"He'll have changed his name, like Jim did," Barry suggested.

"Could be. Making himself still more open to blackmail. I'll
have to ask Uncle Will. He may still know Roy's home
address. If he comes up with anything useful I'll let you know,
Barry. You'll have to do the research. I'm tied here for
months, except for the odd weekend."

The journalist agreed and they parted with their new plan of
campaign fixed, not at all hopeful of results, but determined to
persevere.

Brigadier Stowden wrote in answer to Colin's letter that he
was very interested to hear the latest news but had grave
doubts that he could be of any help. However, he sent the only
address he had for Roy Waters, dating from nearly thirty
years back. He asked to be kept informed of any progress. He
would like to see Colin again if he was ever in the neighbourhood of Twitbury St Mary. A friendly letter, rambling
gently, possibly helpful, probably not. Barry took the address
without enthusiasm. It led him one morning three days later
to a small town, scarcely more than a village, in the Cotswolds.
At first he thought either Colin or the old soldier had got the
whole thing wrong. There was no house of the name given, no
road either.

After stopping passers-by with no result he asked his way to
the municipal buildings and into the housing department. At
first he met with total indifference and a stern refusal of help.
But by sheer force of will he managed in the end to reach a
senior official who told him, with a face of astonishment, that
the whole of the district he mentioned had been demolished
nearly eight years before to make way for a council housing
estate.

"Then you don't know if the family I'm looking for moved to another house in the town or left the neighbourhood altogether?"

"Have you looked in the telephone directory?"

"Of course I have. There are half a dozen Waters. But I don't know the first name of the people I want, so that doesn't help."

"You don't know much about them at all, do you?"

"That's why I'm here," said Barry.

The senior official took this as a piece of impertinence.

"I'm afraid I can't help you," he said disapprovingly. "Have you tried the police?"

"I was keeping them to the end," Barry answered untruthfully and went away, hoping the other would not report him as a loiterer with intent.

Back in the High Street Barry considered his position. Obviously the town had changed very much in the last eight years, but that was not so very long ago. If Roy Waters's family had lived there until the council project started or just before it, surely some of the townspeople would remember them. The shopkeepers, the clergy, perhaps. He remembered passing a church, built in Victorian gothic, on his way to the area where the house and road he sought had been swallowed up.

Here he was partly successful. The present vicar was an elderly man, a late entrant to the ministry. He had not lived in the town before he took over his parish, but he was interested in its history. He was quite willing to show Barry the registers, where they found the entry of Roy Waters's birth and baptism. His parents had then been living at the address Barry held. Even more helpful was a record of the father's death in 1957.

"The churchyard runs along the boundary of the new estate," the vicar said. "Perhaps I should have put that the other way round. There is a gap in the wall, bricked in now, where a gate led into the vicarage garden next door. The old

vicarage has gone too, of course. But I should not have wanted
to live in such a big, rambling place. I have a house on the
estate. Much better. We know our parishioners that way."

He went with Barry to the churchyard where, after some
searching, they discovered the Waters grave. Robert, husband
of Rachel, deceased, aged seventy-two years. Robert, who had
fathered Roy thirty-six years before. Where did Rachel, the
mother, lie? Rachel, deceased. So both the parents were gone.
There was no mention of Roy nor of any other child.

Armed with these basic facts Barry was encouraged to go on
with his search. The shops came next, he decided.

But here he had less success. The two big self-service stores
were out of it altogether, he thought. The new estate had a
row of new shops; there were none between the church and the
main streets of the town. One or two old-fashioned butchers,
grocers, and fishmongers seemed well patronised. They stood
in a row of mid-eighteenth century houses that might have
been private dwellings when they were built, but had de-
scended to trade in Victorian times. One grocer remembered
the Waters family clearly. Mr Waters had continued to be his
customer after his wife died.

"And the son?" Barry asked, handing over the money for
the unwanted goods he had bought.

"Used to make up a bag of sweets for him when he was a
nipper, time and time again. Never came here much after the
war. National Service didn't suit him, so Mr Waters always
said. I believe he went for a doctor. I don't rightly remember.
Best part of twenty year back, now."

"None of the family still in the neighbourhood, then?"

"Oh no, sir. There weren't but the three of them any time.
He sold the house and garden for the estate. Don't know where
he went. But they brought him back to his wife's grave in the
end. Changed the headstone, too. I wouldn't know who did
that. I disremember."

"I thought you said he stayed on after Mrs Waters's death?"

The grocer eyed him suspiciously.

"So he did. A twelvemonth, maybe. I disremember that, too. Would you be a friend of the family, sir?"

"Not really," Barry answered, deciding that honesty was his only safeguard at this moment. "A connection of his asked me to make inquiries as I was coming here today."

His purchases were in a carrier bag, his bill paid. Barry tucked his briefcase under his arm and with the carrier bag swinging, thanked the grocer and walked out of the shop, nearly colliding, as he reached the door, with a thin man in a dark brown suit.

There was one possibility, he thought as he stood outside, wondering which way to go. Across the road, fixed to a lamp post, a faded, rusting notice, hanging askew, directed would-be passengers to the railway station.

Now Barry knew that the local branch line had recently been closed, for he had been obliged to wait an hour for a country bus when he had been turned out of his London express at the junction, six miles away. But the railway was in use all the time the Waters family lived in the place. Presumably Roy, at least, must have travelled sometimes by train as a boy. The closure had been very recent, he was told at the junction. There might be work of a kind still going on at the station. He determined to find out.

He was right. It would have been difficult to guess that the closure had taken place, he decided, unless you stayed there long enough to despair of any train coming along the still bright rails. Being December, grass had not yet sprung up between the sleepers. The poster boards still carried advertisements of films, foods, holidays in the sun, houses for sale and to let. There was even the usual single porter or handyman, in uniform trousers and an old British warm, sweeping the deserted platform.

Barry approached him, though he knew his mission could have no result here. The chap was younger than himself. But he began his now familiar opening, watching, without expectation, for any likely response.

To his glad surprise it came, well before his elaborations of the main theme were over.

"Not me," the youth said, "that be afore my time. My grandfer'd know, though. He acted station master thirty year an' more. They let him keep the cottage on, till the rails and that is took up. Down end of up platform, sir, little gate into station garden. My granfer got three prizes for that garden, over the years, I mean. We thinks that's for why they let 'im keep it on."

"Which is the up platform?" Barry asked. He was answered by a pointing finger and a gale of laughter at his astonishing ignorance. Slightly offended he said, 'thank you' in a haughty voice and walked away.

"You can cross the rails," the youth yelled after him. "Never had no electricity here and there bain't no train coming."

The laughter rang out again, so Barry affected not to hear and walked to the end where he found the proper crossing. As the cottage gate was exactly opposite him when he climbed the further slope, he felt justified in not taking the boy's mocking advice.

The ex-stationmaster was gracious. Life had become very boring since they closed the line. He still had the garden, but without the competition there didn't seem much point in working hard at it. Especially as he was likely to be turned out when they found some other use for the railway property. He'd be glad to go, he said. Besides, his wife found it too quiet; unnatural she found it, without the trains running though. Specially of a night time. The Waters family? Yes. Young Roy. A bit of a lad, in some ways. Went for a doctor; very keen on the work at first. Didn't stick to it. Let on at home he was still at the hospital— But there, National Service didn't do him no good."

"D'you mean he left off studying and didn't let his family know?"

"That's right. I never properly got the hang of it. Kept them in ignorance best part of a month, so I was told. But he was only home once in that time. Before that he come down most weekends, regular. But after that last time he never come no more. Folk talked a lot, spread rumours he was in all kinds of trouble. Wrong, of course. Mrs Waters said to me once when I inquired after him, 'He's gone abroad, Ben. We shan't see him for a long time'. She always called me Ben, having knowed me when I was first took on as a porter here. She said it in a hopeless sort of way and I don't mind telling you I didn't believe her. It's my belief he just took himself off—didn't write— Must have had a queer streak somewhere."

"He must," Barry agreed. "Studied at a medical school, did he, when he left the army? D'you know which one? In London, was it?"

"Oh yes, London," the old man answered, without hesitation. "St Edmunds. I never forget that because Mr Roy advised me to take my daughter there. Child at the time, of course, my girl. Mother of that slapdash young feller over on the down platform you was talking to."

This seemed to make up the sum of the stationmaster's knowledge, so Barry thanked him, admired the garden a second time and went away.

He had to wait in the town for the next bus to the junction. They went every hour, he was told, but had no connection with any particular train there. As usual the schedule was worked out for the convenience of the bus crews, not that of the passengers.

Barry found himself alone when he boarded the bus. He had been the only person waiting at the stop and on arrival the crew had left it for a ten minute break. Before they came back, however, two more passengers arrived; a pleasant-faced country woman with a big empty shopping basket and a tall thin man in a dark brown suit.

Barry stared at the brown trousers for several seconds before remembering that he had seen them before that day. Nothing remarkable in that. A very usual type of coincidence. It was not until he found himself, two hours later, again facing the brown suit as his express train from Reading reached the suburbs of London that he took another close look at the owner of the suit and did not much like what he saw. The man had a lean, lined face, dark circles of exhaustion or worry under his eyes, a tight-lipped mouth turning down at the corners.

Disillusioned, disappointed, possibly dangerous, Barry said to himself, choosing the alliterative words on purpose. He stared at the man quite openly, hoping to force upon him the fact that he was aware the other had followed him on his day's research.

The stranger met his gaze without flinching; even with a sort of arrogant amusement. As there were other people in the carriage Barry felt he had nothing to fear. So he turned his head away after a time to watch the houses and streets thicken and blacken, the lights multiply in the fading light of the December afternoon. At Paddington he got out of the carriage last, collecting his overcoat and briefcase from the rack above his seat. He pulled on the coat before leaving the carriage, but left it unbuttoned as he felt for his return ticket in an inner pocket of his jacket.

After passing the barrier he fastened the overcoat and thrust his hands into the pockets, holding the briefcase under one arm. There was a piece of paper in the lefthand pocket that had not been there before. He did not take it out until he boarded the train at Waterloo that would take him to Brackenfield. Then he unfolded it. Amateurish, stupid, melodramatic, he thought, but quite consistent with brown suit's general appearance.

'Jim Sparks deserved all he got,' the note read. 'Let dead curs lie. Keep out.'

When he arrived at Brackenfield, Barry took a taxi to the hospital to find Colin. The next move would be up to his friend.

CHAPTER SIXTEEN

Colin agreed. He was disturbed by the news that Barry had been followed during his researches in Roy Waters's home town. But it was obvious that they must be on the right track again, for only Roy himself, or someone who knew of his early friendship with Jim, would have been so sure of Barry's mission. The note was not only a warning; it was an outpouring of fanatical emotion, even a kind of confession. It was also a bit of a nonsense, Colin thought, not at all the sort of thing Alec Hilton's mob would think up. Their warnings came with blows, with knuckle-dusters or knives. Not with well-expressed correctly spelled notes, introduced quietly into overcoat pockets in trains.

Colin rang up St Edmunds Hospital in London and asked to make an appointment to see the dean of the medical school. He gave his name and standing and his former medical school, which was not St Edmunds. The cautious female voice at the other end asked for his address, said she would ring back. This she did not do, but a letter arrived from the dean, agreeing to see Dr Frost the following Saturday morning as he understood the registrar would not be free at any other time.

"Very decent of him," Colin explained to Barry, "seeing he probably never goes in at the weekend. Our chap never did."

"Dean?" Barry asked. "D'you mean clergyman?"

Colin laughed. "By no means. Medical as the rest of the staff. One of the seniors. Donkey work all done by women like the one who suspected me of evil intentions on the phone yesterday."

"Very funny. You give me stitches. What does a medical dean *do*, for Pete's sake?"

"Gets the low-down on each and every one of the un-

qualified students. Arranges their work, which firm they're to
be on, which of the consultants, which of the housemen. That
sort of thing."

"Not altogether clear, but I think I get. I can see he would
be the right bloke to go to."

"That's why I'm going, you nit."

The dean of St Edmunds medical school was polite, but
vague. At least to begin with. When he had heard the whole of
Colin's story, with the full medical detail, he sat silent for a
few seconds, then sprang to his feet and left the room.

Colin waited, gazing round the walls where hung photo-
graphed groups of stalwart young men clutching bats, foot-
balls of both shapes, hockey sticks, tennis rackets. The faces
were depressingly similar, only the cut of the blazers or shorts
varied a little from decade to decade. Evidently the dean was
or had been keen on games.

On an impulse Colin got up and wandered from frame to
frame, looking for a face he might recognise. But he did not
find it, so he sat down again. Almost at once the dean returned, carrying a folder.

"Sorry to keep you waiting," he said. "The students' records
department had a face lift last year. Impossible to find what
you want now, of course."

He untied the folder, snapped open the holding clip and
glanced at the two top sheets of the record. He then flapped
over several more, to pick out two towards the bottom of the
meagre pile.

"Roy Sanderson Waters. That the man you want?" he
asked.

"I don't know his middle name."

"Never mind. Only Roy Waters we've had here. Now, let me
see. Matriculated 1945, aged seventeen. Called up 1946.
Left the army 1948. Entered medical school here next year,
autumn."

The dean looked up inquiringly.

"You know all that, perhaps?"

"Only that he left the army in 'forty-eight. There had been some trouble there. Probably you know."

"I do. His father came to me about it. I wasn't going to tell you if you didn't know."

"Sir, please tell me *all* you *do* know. I've told you what—"

"Yes, yes. Attempted murder. Well, now. Waters did well in his pre-clinical work, came out quite high in the exams. I thought very favourably of him when we had him in the wards. Worked hard. Made a few friends. Not altogether popular, no good at games, didn't try, I believe. The trouble began when he was in his second year at the hospital."

"Trouble? The work, d'you mean?"

"His work went off. Definitely. Seemed to lose interest in the whole thing. In himself, too. I suspected drink—or drugs. I met him in a corridor one morning, looking dreadful. Obviously not been to bed the night before, unshaved, dirty, impossible—"

The dean shuddered at the recollection. Colin waited. It was not a moment to interrupt.

"I had him in here and demanded an explanation. He looked absolutely desperate, broke down, said he couldn't go on. I tried to get out of him what the trouble was, but he wouldn't tell me. Just begged me not to write to his father, not yet, he kept repeating. He'd try to put everything right, if only I wouldn't tell his father."

"But he didn't succeed?"

"For a time I thought he had. He went on pretty well till he was into his third year and reading up for the first part of the conjoint. Then he simply disappeared."

"Really? I mean, literally?"

"Quite literally. He was in the hospital one day and not the next. We never saw him here again. He had been home the weekend before and his parents never saw him again after that, either."

"Wasn't any sort of search made?"

"We thought of making one until I had a letter from him.

To begin with I had been afraid of suicide. I still was. His letter simply repeated what he'd said to me before. That he couldn't go on. He was getting out and would stay out. Naturally I took that for a threat of suicide."

The dean put down the papers he held and looked steadily at Colin.

"It was after all this that his father told me about the army scandal. I wish he'd told me before."

"There was a repeat, was there?"

The dean nodded.

"I think there must have been. But if so it never reached me, so someone must have helped him out."

"Was he so short of money, always?"

"No. Certainly not. In the early years. But he was very short that last eighteen months."

"Blackmail, I suppose?"

"Or gambling? Or a girl? Not drink or drugs. We were sure of that before the end, though it had been in my mind at one time, as I told you."

"You must have gone on making inquiries. His friends? Didn't *anyone* know he was in a jam? Or try to help him?"

"I told you someone must have helped him at the end. Not a student, I think. You know what students are? And he had no close friend among them. It's difficult to ask. These are men— not boys. There is a very well defined limit you can't go beyond in trying to force confidences."

Colin agreed. He thought the dean had acted very well on the whole.

"Why did you give up the idea of suicide?"

"Because he wrote once to his father, who told me this. He had gone north, judging from the postmark, found a job of some sort, did not intend to come back and they were to forget him. He gave no address and the postmark did not help."

"I see."

This seemed to mark the end of the dean's usefulness. Colin said, "I'm very grateful for what you've told me. I believe

Waters is alive and may well be the man I'm looking for. If it won't be too much trouble, can you tell me any of his contemporaries, friends or otherwise, who just possibly might know what became of him?"

The dean left the room again and came back with more papers, which he showed to Colin. They were not very helpful. More than twenty students in Waters's first year class had passed their second medical exam and moved on to hospital work. Eighteen of these had qualified. Nine had gone into general practice, two into the medical side of the Services, one into Public Health. The remaining six had stayed on in the hospital service to get higher degrees. Of these, three had emigrated, one had died, the remaining two were consultants.

"Neither of them at this hospital," said the dean wryly. "It seems to have been a very unsatisfactory year from our point of view."

He handed the list, with the notes he had made on it, to Colin.

"You'll have to do your own work on these, if you think it worth while," he said. "Personally I should advise you to leave well, or bad, alone. The blackmailer, if he was one, is dead, I think you told me. If Waters tried to kill him and his medical career was ruined by this man he had a good excuse and is not likely to repeat such a crime. After all, your Indian colleague did make a considerable howler. *He* won't do that again either. He'll live it down. The shortage is far too great for anything drastic to happen to him. Not as if it had been in the ward. The chap was only in out-patients for an hour or two, wasn't he? Dying when he came in. I'd drop it, if I were you."

"You don't know our coroner, sir," Colin said. "Very biased, I'm afraid. Still thinks Patel made up the whole story to cover his gross inefficiency."

He saw that the dean had now lost interest and was waiting for him to go. So renewing his sincere and genuine thanks for the interview he went back to Brackenfield.

During the next few days Colin snatched every slack moment to write to the various names on the list of Waters's sometime fellow students. Of the GPs two answered, the rest ignored his appeal. This was not unexpected. They lived in various parts of the United Kingdom; it was more than fifteen years since they had seen the man. Quite probably he had been no more to them than a face in the wards, a neighbour at table in the refectory, a figure moving around the specimen bottles in the museum or sitting over a book in the medical school library.

The Medical Officer of Health, working in a Midland town, did write, on official paper, typed by a secretary, to say he had shared rooms with Roy Waters from their second, pre-clinical year, but that Roy had moved away some six months before he finally left. This had worried him at the time but he was working for his finals and had done nothing about it. He would like to know Roy's present whereabouts.

The two GPs who answered had no idea where Roy Waters was to be found.

One of the consultants was ill, his wife wrote. She would give him Dr Frost's letter when he was well enough, but the name was unfamiliar. She did not think Mr Waters had been a friend.

The other consultant wrote from a private address in Berkshire to say he would very much like to meet Dr Frost in connection with his inquiry and would like him to come to the address from which he wrote. He hoped this would not be inconvenient. Perhaps Dr Frost would care to come to luncheon and they could talk afterwards. Colin accepted this arrangement with pleasure.

Paul Meadows, surgeon, was an energetic, stocky person, Colin found, an ardent player of golf and tennis. He lived in a large, comfortable house, with an elegant, intelligent wife, and had three children all at boarding school. He worked for a group of hospitals in the region and must be doing well in the private sector, Colin decided, unless he or his wife or both enjoyed private means. He was amused to find later that his deductions were correct.

After an excellent lunch, cooked by Mrs Meadows, her husband suggested a walk, during which they could discuss their business. Colin was only too pleased to agree. Any real exercise made a welcome change in his present life.

"I got your name among others on a list supplied by the dean of St Edmunds," he said, as soon as they were out of earshot of the house.

"I know. He wrote to tell me so."

"Because he knew you were a friend of Waters?"

"Perhaps."

"He didn't tell me he was going to write. Just gave me a list of names of people he said might help."

"Look," Meadows said, turning his head to meet Colin's puzzled stare. "Suppose you tell me what all this is in aid of, first."

Colin hesitated. But as he received no further encouragment he stated his case again, hearing his voice repeat the familiar facts, the all too stale situation, the profitless results of his laborious research. He knew he had condensed and simplified the whole story. He might be reading a script, he thought bitterly.

"And why have you come to me?" Mr Meadows asked at the end of it.

"*Why*? I've told you, or I meant to. Because I'm looking for someone, anyone at all, who knows the real reason for Roy Waters giving up medicine and disappearing."

"Because you think this crook, Sparks, or whatever else he called himself, was at the bottom of it?"

"Naturally."

"You're right. He *was* at the bottom of it, but the real reason, as you call it, was Roy's own weakness. He was corrupted by his own fear, his own over-ruling wish to run away, from the very beginning. He ruined *himself* all along the line."

"This ties in with what we think," Colin answered gravely.

"We?"

"A friend of mine who has done some of the interviewing. I can't get off much. I'm in your line of business, ten years back, I should think."

"Then God help you! Now, you'd better get Roy's record straight. He came to me before they sacked him at St Edmunds—"

"Sacked! But I thought—"

"Don't interrupt! I say he came to me with the whole story. A crook friend who had dragged him into a scandal in the army. How he'd managed to cover that up at his home and to get into St Edmunds. How the crook had located him a few years later and started systematic blackmail."

"Exactly as I thought," Colin could not help exclaiming.

Meadows paid no attention but went on.

"We were in the same year, as you know. He'd always done a bit better than me in written tests, and long cases, but less well in vivas and on spot diagnoses. He began to lose his grip, go down to the bottom of the class, as it were. He was jittery, absentminded, not reading anything like enough. Everyone noticed it. Most people thought he was drinking. He had certainly stepped up the intake, but that wasn't the cause. It was the nagging fear he had of this character who was blackmailing him. And the difficulty of finding the money. He was getting desperate."

"He told you all this?"

"He came to borrow from me. He knew I had a bit laid by. I was a late entry, like him. But I did my stint in the war and got a gratuity. My old man was very generous, too."

A real good luck story, Colin thought. Easy for him to be kind.

"I let him have a bit the first time, but only on condition he told me what the trouble was. When I knew I tried to get him to go to the police. No go. So out came the army scandal. Publicity would ruin his chances of qualifying. I agreed at the time. I wish now I'd gone to the police myself. They knew this

L

Sparks chap by then. But Roy wouldn't do a thing to help himself by getting rid of Sparks."

"Not then," Colin said. "Not until now."

They walked on for a time in silence. Then the surgeon began again.

"I told him, if he wouldn't act for himself, to go to his parents or their solicitor and put the case to them. I don't believe the medical school would have turned him down if he'd made the slightest effort to throw off this—this strangler—for that's what he was."

"But that was no good, either?"

"He said he'd done what I told him, but he hadn't. He'd told his father he was in debt and got the old boy to put up three separate sums to clear him temporarily. All a lie, of course. You can't call blackmail a debt by any stretch of the imagination."

"So then what happened?"

"The crash, of course. Mr Waters wouldn't pay out any more. Roy was broke. The dean was after him because Mr Waters had written to ask what Roy was doing to need so much extra cash. Also because his work had gone to pot."

"Typical, I suppose," Colin agreed. He had come across one case in his own student days. But that had been drugs, a senseless experimenter who got hooked. Practically a nut case by the time he was sent down.

"Roy came to me again," the surgeon went on. "This time I knew it was hopeless. He'd been dipping into the hospital Sports Club fund. He didn't play games, so he thought they wouldn't suspect him. The club treasurer was a friend of his, oddly enough. Or so he said. Perhaps he'd just cultivated him in hopes."

"They don't learn do they?" Colin said, meaning petty thieves and their like.

"He had to learn then and quickly," Meadows said. "Shall we turn back now?"

Colin realised that he had noticed nothing of the countryside on the way out. He would not have known how to get back without a guide. As the surgeon did not seem inclined to speak again he asked, "What did Waters do? What did you do for him?"

"I told him to drop medicine, go away, a long way away, change his name, find a job. I told the dean what he'd done and paid the money back into the Sports fund. The wretched treasurer had been going about looking like death with everyone thinking he'd been helping himself. The whole thing was hushed up pretty successfully. His father was told to invent any story he liked, but advised not to put the police on to finding his son, for obvious reasons. No one saw Roy again."

"Except you," Colin said.

Meadows gave him a quick look, but smiled.

"I've never actually seen him," he said. "But I don't pretend I haven't been in touch. At very long intervals, I may say."

"Would you know what he's doing now?"

"I would. But I'm not going to tell you."

His face changed. It grew red, angry.

"Can't you leave the poor beggar alone?" he cried. "He can't help being a moral coward. He's managed to find a place for himself. He isn't lying. I've checked. He's fairly happy in the work he does. If he did come across the blackmailer again, he never said so to me. You've no proof. You never will have. Leave the poor devil alone. Hasn't he suffered enough in all conscience? Don't you realise how dangerous these inquires of yours might be to him?"

"I realise it now," Colin said.

He was thinking of the warning slipped into Barry's overcoat, of the tall man in the dark brown suit. Roy Waters himself? Or a friend of his? An associate in crime or a partner in some legitimate business?

"I've got to clear Patty with the coroner," he said, thinking aloud.

The surgeon exclaimed in contempt. He repeated the dean's arguments about the Indian's prospects. He did not seem to think a small blight on them would matter very much. He implied that Dr Patel did not matter very much anyway.

"Teach the fellow a very necessary lesson," he said severely. "He'll never make that mistake again. But the wretched Waters can't afford another blow, not a really crippling one, as this would be. The enemy's dead, whether your friend had a hand in it or not. Who are you to hound an innocent man?"

"Who indeed, if he *is* innocent," Colin answered. "But is he? I want to know that. I must find out."

They walked on in a silence broken only by conventional, meaningless remarks. When they reached the house, Colin thanked his host, excused himself from going in again, gave a polite message for Mrs Meadows and with renewed thanks got into his car and drove away.

Why should he spare Roy Waters if the man had made this abominable attempt at murder? Quite as loathsome as the old-fashioned poisonings. Waters was not wholly a victim, anyway. He had partnered Jim Sparks in his early fraud. He had not been forced to do that, or had he already given Jim some handle of dishonesty to turn the screw on him? He had been dishonest since, many times. He had arranged his last theft to incriminate the innocent Sports Club treasurer. He was, in fact, a hardened and habitual criminal, Colin decided, a hopeless case. Even though Sparks was dead, would that be the end? Paul Meadows, surgeon, was a sentimental, middle-aged fool.

The sentimental, middle-aged fool watched the young man drive away, then he went into the house and into his private patients' consulting room, where he locked the door against possible interruptions. He searched his desk for a letter and having found it propped it in front of him, took up the telephone receiver and dialled.

He got through almost at once and listened.

"Yes," he said when he was answered. "My name is Meadows. Paul Meadows."

CHAPTER SEVENTEEN

On the evening after Colin's visit to the surgeon, Barry Summers was brought into the Casualty department of the Brackenfield General with a broken ankle and bruises. He had been knocked down as he was walking along the pavement of one of the back streets of the town. A police constable came with him.

Barry was in no shape to give a coherent story of the accident. Colin, who was called to the case, arranged to admit him at once, had him wheeled off for the injury to be X-rayed and asked the constable what had happened.

"We don't rightly know," the officer answered. "Whatever hit him came up from behind and mounted the pavement. That much he was able to tell us, but he never saw it, he says. I was hoping to ask Mr Summers a few questions, but if you say he mustn't—"

"You didn't see it happen?"

"No, sir. I don't think anyone did. Not clearly. There were people round him when I got to the spot, but they were confused. One man thought he got the car number—"

"A car, was it? Didn't stop, then?"

"No. It didn't stop. All Mr Summers says, and he repeats it, is that he was walking along the pavement and something crashed into him from behind, mounting the kerb, knocking him over and crashing back into the road. Dangerous driving, of course. Mr Summers seems to think it was deliberate, but I can't see it would be that."

"No," Colin said, "I don't suppose you can. I should take your report back to the station and get the car and the owner identified if you can. Look, I'll give you a note for Inspector Rawlinson. He won't be pleased."

Seeing an anxious look appear on the constable's face

he laughed and added, "He won't be pleased with Barry Summers was what I meant. He'll say 'I warned the silly young—' "

"Journalist, isn't he?" the constable said, looking relieved. "They do think they can stick their noses into every darned case that crops up, don't they?"

"Yes," answered Colin. He was writing his note to Rawlinson, no longer paying any attention to the constable's remarks. The latter took the note and went away. Colin went along to the X-ray department to look at the picture of Barry's cracked bones.

Inspector Rawlinson called at the hospital the following morning. Colin had been able to secure a cubicle bed for Barry in the orthopaedic ward, chiefly for privacy. Neither of them wanted the story of the accident spread beyond the nurses who had heard it when he came in. They had been told a very modified tale.

Rawlinson was as severe as the two young men expected, but in spite of this direct blow from the enemy they were both unrepentant.

"I warned you," Rawlinson said, showing that he believed the journalist's story in essence.

"Good," said Barry. His voice was weaker than usual and his face pale from the analgesic drugs he had been given, but the tone was confident. "It was carelessness on my part, I know, but it proves they're on to us."

"Who's they?" the inspector asked.

"That's what we hope you'll tell us," Colin suggested.

Between them they reported their search for Roy Waters or any information about him. Barry described his fellow passenger and the note he had found in his overcoat. Colin reported on all he had discovered at St Edmunds Hospital and from Paul Meadows, the surgeon, Roy's former friend.

"I think he may still be his friend," Colin said finally. "He spoke as if he had followed his career, if you can call it that, right through. He's definitely on his side, in spite of every-

thing. In fact both he and the dean at St Edmunds were cagey
to a degree. The dean told me one lie after another. Or it may
have been Meadows that lied. Hushing up was the line from
both of them.'

"What has this man, Waters, to do with Sparks's death?"
the inspector asked.

"Changed the blood group," Colin said, surprised by the
question. "*You know*. It came up at the inquest. Medical
knowledge. Knew of Sparks's obsession. What I'm wondering
is—could he have been the man in the Hillman, the one with
the knife?"

"He could not," said Rawlinson. "We've got that man and
we've got Clarice Field. Surely you read of their appearance in
the magistrate's court at Brighton? Alec Hilton, remanded in
custody, charged with attempted murder. Clarice Field, on bail
since, charged with withholding information and with failing
to report herself to the police. Bail put up by her brother, Bob
Trueman."

"I'm not surprised," Barry said. "He's got a positive genius,
that kid, for keeping out of trouble. Which probably means
he's got a nice bit put by."

"So it appears," said Rawlinson shortly. He was irritated by
the persistence of these two. Hilton was caught at last with a
charge that would undoubtedly stick. He wanted no inter-
ference, no further confusion in the case.

But Colin was only interested in Roy Waters.

"Then is it possible this man Waters belongs to the gang?"
he asked. "Could it have been Waters that Barry saw on the
bus and the train? He must have had a tip off Barry was going
to his old home town. Who tried to kill Barry yesterday? I
thought the car number was seen by someone. Can't it be
identified?"

"We don't know what kind of vehicle hit Mr Summers," the
inspector said. "The crowd round him had scuffed up any
marks it may have made on the pavement. Occasional traffic
was passing along that street, but no one has come forward, in

spite of a call put out for information. One of the onlookers gave us a car number, but it was no good."

"Why?"

"It belongs to a Rover owned by one of our most respected town councillors," Rawlinson answered. "He agrees he left it outside his garage last night because his father-in-law's car was inside. He agrees his car was not locked, but he had taken the key indoors. The car was in place this morning and he can't find any damage on it anywhere."

"Difficult," said Colin.

"Impossible," said the inspector. "Wrong number, most likely."

Barry said, "I'm not sure now it *was* a car hit me. I think I'd be dead if it had been. I think it may have been a heavy motorbike."

The inspector grunted. He had been coming to that conclusion himself. If only the onlookers had been there earlier— No, then it wouldn't have happened that way. If only several cars had not drawn up to offer help. It hadn't even been raining; the road was bone dry. There was nothing to be got from the marks on it.

Barry said, "Don't you know any other members of that gang, Inspector? Associates, if you'd rather. No photos in your records to show me?"

"Wait," said Colin. "I know where I can get hold of a picture of Roy Waters. Uncle Will showed me one. His nephew and Waters, in army uniform. If he'll lend it to me I'll show it to both of you. Barry can say if it's the chap in the brown suit and the inspector can tell us if he had a record. Right?"

The two men agreed. Barry lay back and shut his eyes, hoping someone would come soon and give him another dose to stop the throbbing in his plastered leg. Colin went about his business in the hospital.

Inspector Rawlinson went back to the police station, curious to see the photograph the registrar was going to secure for him. He was more impressed by the story of Waters's failure to become a qualified doctor than he had allowed himself to show at the hospital. Failed medicos could be a nuisance in many criminal ways, as abortionists, drug pushers, plastic surgeons for villains who wanted their faces changed, emergency men who would treat 'hot' tearaways and not report their injuries to the police, even when asked. He looked forward to getting this man identified.

Colin rang up Brigadier Stowden's house that evening, only to find that the old man had gone to stay with friends and might not be back until after Christmas.

This was serious. They were already into the second week of December, so the housekeeper's opinion had real probability.

"Can you tell me where I could get in touch with him?" he asked.

"Any letter you care to write, sir, will be forwarded," the cautious answer came, and no amount of persuasive argument would change it.

However, on working out dates, Colin realised that he could not in any case get away at the coming weekend, so he wrote a letter, stating as briefly as he could all his latest discoveries and asking permission to show the photograph of Jim and his friend to the police. The answer in the form of a telegram arrived in three days' time. It stated simply, 'Expect you Saturday week seven p.m. Stowden'.

Colin got the telegram as a telephoned message written down at the main porter's lodge of the hospital. He asked for the written copy, which he found stuck into the letter board beside the main doors. He took it up to show Barry.

The latter was less interested in Colin's new project than in the progress of his own case.

"Why can't I go home?" he said. "They make me waggle my toes and move my leg about and do a hell of a lot of frantic exercises. Those physio girls are absolutely inhuman. You could scream your head off and they'd just smile and tell you to repeat the exercise."

"You're safer where you are," said Colin.

"From another bash at writing me off?"

"That for a start. For a good result from the break as well. You don't want to come out of it a limping cripple, do you? Leave it to the orthopods."

He handed the telegram to Barry, who gave it one look of disgust and envy and put it on the top of his locker, from where it was soon blown off by the draught in the ward and floated down to the floor. Later on, when the voluntary help, who assisted at meal times came in with a tray for Barry she saw the yellow slip and picking it up while he was lifting covers to see what he had been given to eat, put it in her pocket and took it away.

Colin planned to get off early on Saturday afternoon in order to enjoy a pleasant drive in the country while the light lasted, followed by refreshment in some well-warmed tea room before going on to the brigadier's house near Twitbury St Mary.

This programme, as so many others in Colin's present life, was ruined by the arrival of a perforated gastric ulcer case, very ill, whose family had not wanted to disturb their own doctor in the middle of the previous night. Nor had they suggested, when at last they called him, that the case was urgent. Consequently it came to Colin in the middle of his lunch and by the time he had admitted the man, operated upon him, revived him, watched him and later pronounced him safe enough for a few hours to leave in the care of his second in command, it was half-past five, with Uncle Will expecting him in an hour and a half.

It was then that one of his friends said, "You'll never make it in that old crock of yours. Why not take mine? I'm stuck here for the evening."

"D'you mean that?"

"Why not? You passed your test, didn't you?"

This friendly gesture, quite uncalled for, Colin always afterwards declared had saved his life. Though he was never able to prove it.

He had driven the small, low-slung sports car on several previous occasions, which was probably why its owner trusted him with it. He knew his route, the sports car's lights were excellent. There was a good deal of traffic on the main roads, but the side turnings which he used habitually at weekends both for overall speed and comfort were nearly deserted. He passed through Twitbury St Mary at ten minutes to seven.

The brigadier's house lay in a narrow lane that looked wider than it was because no hedges hemmed it in. For part of the way there was rough scrub on either side, mainly gorse and blackberry bushes. For a hundred yard strip in the middle young oaks and chestnuts stood among the undergrowth, some growing at the very edge of the trees.

Colin, seeing the darker patch before him, switched on the sports car's very powerful searchlight. He saw, glittering in its beam, a thin wire stretched across the road.

Though he braked on the instant, he knew he could not stop in time. But he saw, with surprise and relief, that the wire appeared to rise as he approached and he understood why. The sports car, so low, so near the ground, would pass underneath. With this fact assured he took his foot from the brake and shot forward again, crouching in his seat, praying that the shining thread would not drop to catch him before he was clear.

There was a fraction of a second's suspense when the light went ahead and the menace, so clearly seen before, was blotted out in darkness. Then the thing was behind and the car, with Colin shaken but thankful, roared away into the distance.

As soon as he had disappeared a watcher in the wood, cursing, uncertain, fearful, took down his trap. He saw that it was too dangerous to risk keeping it up any longer. The car he had waited for had not come. It would be frightful to catch and wreck a stranger. He had failed. He dared not stay there any longer for the one who was late or who was not even on the road. Miserably he took his motorbike from where he had hidden it among the bushes and rode away.

Meanwhile Colin had arrived at the brigadier's house and was given a hearty welcome.

"You look frozen, my boy," Uncle Will said, settling his guest in front of the blazing log fire. "No heater in that vintage car of yours, I suppose?"

Colin explained. The borrowed sports car belonged to a very hardy character who never had the hood up. He had not had time to alter this before starting.

"It was providential I didn't," he explained, describing the hazard on the road.

Brigadier Stowden said, "Good God!" staring at Colin in horror. "You didn't stop?"

"Hadn't time. I braked of course and slowed up a lot. I wasn't going much over fifty, the road's too narrow. But I couldn't have stopped in time and I saw I'd be clear—just."

"I meant stop to find out what the wire was. Take it down and so on."

"And get myself clobbered by the type who fixed it? No thank you."

Uncle Will looked very grave.

"I was going to offer you sherry. But I think you should have whisky—a double."

Colin grinned and accepted. His knees had felt a bit weak ever since he climbed carefully out of the car in the brigadier's drive.

"Now tell me what you've really come for?" Uncle Will said.

Colin explained the progress of his and Barry's investigations, how they had come to the conclusion that Jim's prime enemy must have been his former friend and later victim, Roy Waters. Also that Inspector Rawlinson was quite prepared to follow up anything definite they could offer him.

"You see," Colin went on, "if Waters did go for a life of crime, when he was booted out of medicine, he may at some time have slipped up, got a conviction, got put on the records. We need a photo of him to match up and I know you've got one, sir. You showed it to me, didn't you?"

Without a word Brigadier Stowden produced the photograph and took it over to Colin's chair.

"No, don't get up," he said. "Have another look at it. You said something about Jim's face being familiar. I took it you meant you recognised him from the short time you had charge of him. Which means he didn't change much with the years. I always noticed that, too."

"Yes," Colin said. "I still find the face familiar. I didn't think he was so tall, though. But I only saw him lying down and that's very deceptive over height, as I expect you know."

Uncle Will was astonished.

"But Jim wasn't tall," he said. "You've got them mixed up. Roy's the tall one, by a good four inches. Bit of a maypole, we always thought, Jim and I. Never told him so. Easily offended."

Colin had risen in his excitement. He was still holding the photograph, staring at those features, that long face, long legs —

"I *do* know him," he cried. "I swear I do! In Brackenfield — it must be. Older, of course. What an idiot I am — I just can't place him!"

"Calm down," Uncle Will ordered, pushing Colin gently back into his chair. "No good getting steamed up over this. Sort it out quietly. Your newspaper friend was followed and warned by a tall, thin individual, whom he did not recognise. Right. Possibly Roy. You located a surgeon who had kept in touch with Roy. You were intended to crash your car on the way here to tell me all about it."

"And would have crashed if I hadn't switched cars at the last minute."

"Exactly. Isn't it obvious this person who may be Roy has some very close connection with your hospital, to know so much about your doings. Have you considered who this might be? Obviously not one of the doctors, but someone, always supposing he really is Roy, who might be in touch, or has the help of one of the staff, nursing or domestic, I mean."

"Mr Meadows probably told him about me," Colin said gloomily. "He tried hard to make me give up trying to locate Roy."

"It begins to tie up, doesn't it?"

Brigadier Stowden was at his desk, looking for an envelope in which to put the photograph. Having found one he went back to Colin.

"Now," he said. "Put it in here. You're going to take it to Inspector Rawlinson just as soon as you're fit to do so."

Colin jumped up again.

"I'm perfectly fit now," he said. "You're right, of course. The law must take over action. I'm not suicidal."

"Glad to hear it," Uncle Will told him, stumping towards the door. "But you're not starting till you've got some food in your stomach to mop up that whisky or we'll both be breaking the law. When did you last eat?"

"Don't remember," said Colin, who found the room a trifle misty now and the brigadier's voice reaching him from some distance away. "Lunch, I think. Halfway through, actually. I never got back to it."

"Come along then," Uncle Will encouraged him. "You'll have to take pot luck. I wasn't expected back till after Christmas and I'm leaving again tomorrow night."

An hour later Colin was on his way back to Brackenfield, the photograph stowed in an inside pocket. The brigadier had given him a different route from the one he had come by. It took him a few miles out of his way, but led by unfrequented lanes to a main road further east which took him into the London dual carriageway three miles from Brackenfield.

When Colin reached the police station he found Rawlinson already there.

"Your Brigadier Stowden rang us up after you left to tell us to be ready for you," the inspector said. "Army brass! They never lose the manner, do they?"

"He's been particularly good to me," Colin said. "I suppose he told you what I was bringing you?"

"He told our sergeant on Inquiries a whole lot he hadn't a clue about. But he'd got my name and he repeated his orders at least three times. So they brought me down here and I hope it's been worth it."

Colin handed over the photograph.

"I haven't shown it to Barry yet," he said. "I thought you'd better take charge from now on."

"You did, did you? Darned good of you. Learned your lesson at last?"

Colin had an answer ready but he never gave it, for the inspector had given a short sharp exclamation and was sitting with the photograph in his hand, staring at it with a grim certainty in his eyes.

"You know him, then?" Colin asked. "He really is Roy Waters? He really does have a record?"

"I know him," Rawlinson said, heavily. "What a mess! What an unholy bloody mess!"

Colin stayed in bed late next morning. He reached the residents' dining room after clearing had begun, but managed to find a few dried-up remains on the hot plate and some tepid coffee. He did not linger over this unappetising meal but went as soon as possible to the orthopaedic ward where he found Barry propelling himself around in a wheel chair, visiting and chatting with other sufferers whose injuries tied them to various pieces of complicated machinery attached to their beds.

Colin wheeled him off to his cubicle to give him the news. Barry had heard much of it already.

"That copper came in this morning, early," he explained. "Showed me the picture. Our tall thin man all right. Said he was surprised I hadn't recognised him. Wouldn't tell me why. Wanted to know if I'd been gossiping about the case here in hospital."

"That was because he wanted to know how Waters knew I was going out to Twitbury yesterday."

"So he said. I hadn't a clue."

"What did you do with my telegram? I left it with you."

"Christ!" Barry dived for his locker, searched unsuccessfully. "I swear it was here. Or did I leave it out on top?"

"Stop flapping. Who came in after I left?"

"No one. Yes. The VAD with the eats. You don't think—?"

But Colin had gone, to get Rawlinson on the phone and report the disappearance of the brigadier's telegram. The VAD—

"Or the porter who took the post office message by phone," said Rawlinson. "Or the one who put it up on the letter board. Or anyone interested, who took a look while it was there."

"O.K." said Colin. "I've retired from the fray, you know that. I'm not having anything to do with it until you get the chap and need my evidence."

"Evidence of what?" Rawlinson's voice was scornful.

"Attempted murder—three times. Changing that blood group. Running down Barry. Putting a wire across the road to wreck my car."

"Suspicions. Unsubstantiated so far. Motive, yes. I'll give you that. Opportunity—prove it. Presence at the spot at the times of the incidents? Prove that, too."

"You prove it," Colin said. "I've given you quite enough to work on. I've opted out, I tell you."

But he was wrong again. In the middle of that Sunday afternoon he was called to Casualty. A serious accident. A woman, trying from an upper window to retrieve her child's toy which had fallen on to the glass roof of a conservatory below, had over-balanced and crashed through the glass, cutting herself severely in many parts of her face, arms, shoulders and back.

Colin met Ahmed Patel in the corridor, carrying a bottle of blood. As in a nightmare of repeated disaster Colin's mind went back to that other emergency, so many weeks ago. He was so disturbed by this that he asked sharply, "You've got the right stuff? Test, cross-matching, everything?"

"I would not be likely to make a slip-up again," Patel said, looking hurt.

"Sorry, Patty. I'm a bit on edge."

The scene in Casualty was the same. A cluster of figures round the trolley, staff nurse, junior nurse—or was she a VAD—the ambulance men, a porter—had he been there that other time—an unmoving, supine figure, bandaged—another figure, tall, thin, in a mackintosh and felt hat. Not Rawlinson this time.

As the two doctors approached, all the standing figures straightened, all the faces turned in their direction. And Colin saw at last the face of the photograph, the unmistakable face of Roy Waters. He understood why Rawlinson knew the man and had been upset by his knowledge, he understood and cursed his failure to realise all the time, how Jim Sparks, who had whispered about his diary, had been destroyed by it.

It was a couple of hours before Colin was free to take any action. He and Patel worked on the casualty while a bed in a surgical ward was secured and prepared for her. She was a healthy, young, strong woman, who soon began to respond to their treatment, to recover from the shock and haemorrhage. When there was no longer any doubt of her immediate recovery, Colin left Patel in charge and went away to telephone. After that he went up to Barry's cubicle.

"I've found Roy Waters," he said.

"Who?"

"Ambulance man. Gibson. Joe Gibson."

"But that's *fantastic!* Are you sure?"

Colin was suddenly furious. All the strain and uncertainty of the last weeks broke into rage, chiefly with himself.

"Isn't it obvious, *more* than obvious? Aren't we both utter bloody fools? What have we found, all along the line? *At every step?* That Jim hung on to that blood group as a kind of charm, talked about it, brooded over it, was obsessed by it. So wouldn't he check with that diary, look at the blessed thing, every day, every night, certainly every time he drove a car? Would he have said his blood group was in his diary unless he *knew* it was? The correct one? Of course he wouldn't."

M

"He damn well wouldn't when he saw Roy Waters coming at him with the stretcher."

"He never saw Roy that night. He spoke to the driver—Watts, I think his name is. He was unconscious from then on. Joe Gibson was with Jim, alone with him, in the ambulance. Gibson altered the group letters, Gibson gave Patty the diary. Why did we never stop to work all this out?"

Barry shook his head. People whose job is to save life don't usually plan to take it. He held back the trite remark. Instead he asked anxiously, "Did this chap know you'd recognised him."

"Possibly. Yes, I think very possibly. He got out of the cubicle at once. But then Staff was showing them all out, husband as well." He paused, then said, "I've rung up Uncle Will—and Rawlinson."

"Good," said Barry. "I think I'll have a word with my editor. This seems to be the end of the road. I'll have to make sure there's room in tomorrow's paper for my story."

"Oh God," Colin said, weary and disgusted. "I wish to heaven I'd never begun it."

CHAPTER EIGHTEEN

Brigadier Stowden did not go back to his friends' house on Sunday. After Colin telephoned that morning with his painful, almost unbelievable news, the old man made fresh arrangements, then went to his desk and began a long, unhappy search into those records of the past that he had kept there.

By lunch time he had collected together those letters from Jim he had not hitherto brought himself to destroy. He read them carefully, finding in the earlier ones all the charm that had originally attracted him to his nephew, and in the later all the trust in and exploitation of the affection he had built up. Deliberately? Callously? Uncle Will winced at the

thought, which was not new, but which hit him again most
mercilessly as he read on and on. Before going to his lunch the
old man piled the letters on to his fire, poked them into a
blaze, then fed on some small logs to make sure of their complete destruction.

In the early afternoon he sorted out various receipts and
cheque counterfoils and bank statements that recorded the
rescue operations he had performed for Jim. He had kept
them, too, he now realised, in his permanent hope, never to be
fulfilled, that the boy, as he continued to think of him, would
in the end reform, 'settle down' as he invariably put it to
himself.

That had not happened. There was no longer any point in
keeping a tally of Jim's debts. He knew he had really written
them off years ago. Those loans had been a kind of blackmail
too, he thought now, rubbing salt into the old wounds. The
price of holding his own spurious position of favourite, much-
loved uncle. Self-deception added to Jim's automatic, in-built
power to deceive. A rotten lot, the Stowdens, he thought, but
then remembered those earlier soldiers who had won distinc-
tion in the field and died there, too, most of them.

His housekeeper, bringing in tea on a tray, found him still
at the desk, one lamp only beside it, a pile of paper ash
choking the fire. She set things to rights at once, put the tray
on its usual small table beside the armchair, restored the fire,
switched on more light as she left the room. Which she did
shaking her head over the master's depression, as she called it
to herself. Sipping her own brew in her neat sitting room next
to the old-fashioned kitchen, she heard the telephone bell ring
and hoped the call was from friends and would cheer him
up.

The call was not from friends, but the old soldier was his
normal brisk self when the housekeeper went to his room
again to take away the tray.

"I'm expecting a gentleman at any time in the next two
hours," he said, smiling at her. "There will be other visitors,

too, who may come before or after the gentleman. But just
show 'em all in to me here, whatever order they arrive in."

"Very good, sir," said the housekeeper. The instructions, the
master's recovery, must indeed be the result of that telephone
call. On a Sunday afternoon, too. She felt slightly scandalised.

The single arrival came first. The housekeeper opened the
door, announced, "Mr Gibson, sir," admitted the visitor and
retreated, shutting the door behind her.

Brigadier Stowden came forward, but he did not hold out
his hand.

"Roy!" he said. "After all these years. Well, come and sit
down."

Roy Waters moved into the room, but he did not take the
offered chair.

"Do you really recognise me?" he asked in a low voice, "or
have you been warned I was coming?"

"Both," said the brigadier cheerfully, seating himself again.
"Sit down."

It was an order, unmistakably an order, and Waters obeyed
it, though against his will.

"I see you are in mufti," went on Stowden, looking with
interest at the dark brown suit.

"Why not?"

"Only that I know you work in the St John Ambulance
Corps and that you call yourself Joe Gibson. You gave that
name, Gibson, to my housekeeper, didn't you?"

Roy's face twisted in anger.

"Was it you, then, tipped off that devil?"

"If you mean Jim—no. I only learned it today. But did Jim
know?"

"He always knew."

"I think he cannot have known you were in Brackenfield.
He never approached you there, did he?"

"No. But he could have known. He came to Brackenfield. To
that club. He could have seen me. I never saw him. I thought I
was safe from him, God help me!"

He began to splutter, confused, fearful. A pitiful sight, the brigadier thought, but not one to arouse his own pity.

"Of course he didn't know you were there," he said. "If he'd known that would he have trusted you after the accident?"

"It was Tom he spoke to."

"I see. You took advantage of an unconscious man to alter the blood group in his diary. You couldn't even kill him openly."

Waters stared, his face whitening.

"Dr Frost! I was right then! He *was* at the bottom of this! He's the one's been hounding me, as Paul said— He told you! You can't deny it! But he can't prove a thing! No one can prove a thing!"

The brigadier stopped him with another curt order and when the babbling stopped, spoke in a gentler voice.

"Why have you come here, Roy? You knew perfectly well I have been in touch with young Frost. You tried to stop him, kill him, perhaps. What d'you want?"

"Money. I've got to get out. I saw the look on Frost's face this morning. I'm quitting. For good. Now. Abroad. I need money."

He was on his feet again, his face threatening, his voice rising.

"Do you imagine I keep money in the house?" Uncle Will was calm, but watchful. "The sort of money *you* want."

"You can arrange it. You can send it. I'll tell you where."

"What can you do to me that might induce me to give you money? You can't frighten me, you know. I'm too old to mind dying."

"I can drag your name in the mud! I can—"

"No. Don't pull out all the usual clichés. You can do nothing, Roy. I have no record of any dealings, any communications I ever had with Jim. I have burned the lot. I can deny all knowledge of him, beyond the fact that he was my brother's son. There is no family to care what you say. My name is quite safe with my friends."

"You know what he did to me!"

"I know what you have done to yourself. You could have put him away for blackmail years ago, but you were too cowardly. Don't pretend you paid up for your family's sake or mine. You chose to steal. When you couldn't scrounge you have always stolen. It wasn't blackmail that broke your medical career, it was dipping in the Sports Fund at your hospital. You're running away again now, breaking your new career. Money. You don't want my money. Where have you robbed now?"

"The Ambulance Christmas Fund," said Inspector Rawlinson, from the doorway.

Waters spun round, and now the hand that had been thrust into his pocket had a gun in it. He fired directly he saw the two men standing in the open doorway. He fired and the bullet passed between the two figures as they dropped to the floor. It shattered the glass of a picture in the hall and the housekeeper, who had felt it whistle through her hair as she crossed back from the front door, screamed loudly.

A moment later Roy found himself flying through the air to land heavily on his back, while the brigadier, panting from his unaccustomed exertion, picked up the pistol.

The two detectives recovered first and pounced on Waters, who had been winded by his fall and was in no shape to resist.

"Shall I take that, sir?" Rawlinson then said, holding out his hand for the pistol.

"No," Brigadier Stowden answered. "I think I'll keep it. For the present, anyway. I suppose you thought you were making a diversion, coming in like that without being announced. Ridiculous. You jolly nearly got yourselves shot. Not to mention my housekeeper, who is making so much noise I feel she cannot be seriously injured."

With that he walked out of the room to reassure her and relieve his own anxiety on her behalf.

He was back almost at once. Waters, who now seemed to be

on the point of collapse, stood speechless between the two detectives. Stowden noticed that he was not handcuffed.

"I don't think he'll give us any trouble now," Rawlinson said, as if he referred to an idiot child. "Eh, Joe? You'll come along down to the station and tell us all about it, won't you?"

Waters stared at the ground and did not answer.

"No," said the brigadier, turning his eyes from the captive ruin. "No, I'm sure he won't."

He watched the three men pass through the door, Rawlinson with a hand, a sympathetic hand, the brigadier thought, on the shoulder of his stumbling prisoner.

The police car drove away. Brigadier Stowden lowered himself into his armchair. He had learned judo in the old days to protect himself because he was a short man and sensitive about it. He had not lost the art. He had floored Waters. Was that a revenge, a personal revenge, for Jim's death? He shrank from the thought, rubbing his now aching shoulder.

In the police car, on a fast straight stretch of main road, Waters, sitting beside Rawlinson in the back, suddenly gasped, "I feel sick," lurched at the rear door, flung it open and dived out. He died before the police car stopped.

Alec Hilton was sent for trial at Sussex Assizes on three charges, first the manslaughter of Ivan Totteridge, alias James Sparks, by causing a car smash in which the latter received injuries from which he died; secondly the attempted murder by stabbing of Clarice Field in the said car; thirdly the attempted murder of Clarice Field on the sea front at Brighton.

He was found guilty on all these counts and sentenced to the maximum penalty on each, the sentences to run consecutively which therefore amounted to a considerable retirement from his long-standing war on his fellow men. The police of all the forces involved were delighted with the result. Clarice Field, the most valued witness for the prosecution, was discharged from all her pending trouble. Bob Trueman was congratulated for his devotion to his sister.

Since the matter of Jim Sparks's death had been settled in a court of law, the inquest upon it at Brackenfield was not resumed, so the coroner there had no further opportunity to blacken Ahmed Patel's reputation and the whole medical story was soon forgotten except at the hospital, where it became, with embellishments, a slightly ribald legend among junior staff.

The inquest upon Roy Waters, alias Joe Gibson, was brief and merciful. The manner of his death was not in doubt. He had died of a broken neck and severe head injuries, sustained by falling from a police car travelling at considerable speed. He was, at the time, assisting the police in certain inquiries they were making. Evidence was given that he had complained in the car of feeling sick, had immediately opened the rear door beside him and fallen through it before he could be prevented from doing so.

The coroner, who had heard a few more details from Inspector Rawlinson with regard to Roy's past and the question of the Christmas Fund, decided it would not be in the public interest to publish a private lapse by a member, now dead, of an honourable and honoured body of men. He found the death due to misadventure and left the gossips to argue to their hearts' content in favour of suicide.

This mild conspiracy of silence covered the Brackenfield General as well. No one tried to find out who it was that had warned Roy that his past was being unfolded stage by stage. No one seemed to be particularly distressed by his death, though everyone was shocked. Appropriate letters of condolence and sympathy went out to the Ambulance Headquarters from the Management Committee, the Medical Staff, the Matron on behalf of the nurses and the Head Porter on behalf of his colleagues and himself.

The *Brackenfield Mercury* printed one or two letters of appreciation from former casualties, who had been helped by Joe Gibson. Also a similar letter from the mayor and corporation. Since the man had lived alone, had no known living relative and none came forward after his death, his funeral. a cremation, was sparsely attended and very modestly furnished. All of Barry's sensational story regarding the blood group went unused, but his editor made up for its loss with a full scale account of Hilton's trial, criminal activities and association with Amos Gregson. The club's licence was cancelled, the place closed and Gregson with his family went into the retirement he had planned, though not quite on the luxurious scale he had hoped for.

Colin, arranging Barry's discharge from hospital, expressed satisfaction with all these arrangements.

"Pleased, are you?" Barry said. "What about my leg?"

"*What* about it?"

"Didn't I get it wrecked in a good cause? To get Waters booked for attempted murder? And instead my story goes for a burton and I don't even get compensation. They don't pin anything on him, not *anything*."

"We did what we meant to do," Colin answered. "We solved that blood group mystery and Patty's in the clear. You should see him. He's a different man since last week."

"I have seen him," Barry answered. "He came up to thank me. So, by the way, did old Rawlinson."

"What for, for Pete's sake?"

"Not blowing the whole tale, I think. They always fought shy over the blood group lark, didn't they? He said they wouldn't have used it in the Waters case, either. He'd been raiding the Christmas Fund, but that would never come out because the loss had been made good, anonymously."

"Rawlinson told you! You amaze me. He actually *trusted* you with a story like that?"

Barry grinned.

"He'd squared my editor already. Gave him all the lowdown on Greg's club, the protection angle, all that didn't come out at Hilton's trial."

"Did he say who was the anonymous donor to the raided fund?"

"No. But I can guess. Can't you?"

It was the middle of January before Colin saw the brigadier again. He was invited to lunch and asked to bring Barry Summers and Ahmed Patel with him. This he did, calming the initial fears of the other two, who had preconceived, ignorant ideas, based on the usual caricature of the old-fashioned blimp.

The party went very well. Patel was delighted with Uncle Will's wide-ranging knowledge of his country. Barry was impressed by an outlook and simplicity so entirely unlike anything he had experienced before.

All three young men listened with awe to the brigadier's bland description of his final encounter with Roy Waters. They inspected the bullet hole in the hall.

"Smashed one of my pictures," Brigadier Stowden said. "Nearly got my housekeeper. Not to speak of the two cops. I must say they got down very smartly."

"While you threw Waters and took the gun," Barry said. "Inspector Rawlinson told me. Marvellous."

"The instinct of self-preservation doesn't die with old age, you know," Uncle Will told him, smiling.

When they were about to leave the brigadier kept Colin back.

"I just want to thank you, Colin," he said. "You've done more for me than you know by bringing out the total story of Jim and the crook Hilton and that miserable lad, Roy. Bad hats, the lot of them, but Jim died fighting. He was a proper soldier; had it in the blood, I suppose. Don't know where the flaw came from. But he died fighting to save that girl. That redeems him as far as I'm concerned. See what I mean?"

Colin saw and nodded. But he did not agree. Jim had done too much irreparable damage in his totally self-regarding life.

The brigadier went out with Colin to the drive where Barry and Patel were standing by the registrar's old car.

"Did you tell the owner of that sports car he nearly lost it?" Uncle Will asked.

"No," answered Colin, laughing. He looked at Barry and added, "Another good story down the drain."

"There'll be others," Barry answered. "Wonderfully inventive race we are, aren't we?"

They all thanked the brigadier and got into the car. He leaned in to say a last word to Colin.

"Come and see me sometimes," he said. "I'd like to know how you're getting on. Keep me up to the advance of medicine, you know. The chemistry of crime and all that."

He laughed as he saw Colin redden. Then, standing upright as the car moved away, raised his hand in a formal salute.

Other thrillers by Josephine Bell

THE CATALYST

"Downtrodden husband Hugh accompanies frightful wife and sister-in-law to Greece on holiday, falls for amiable slightly simple actress, decides to cut violently free of family entanglements. Realistic crime story with cunning twist at the end."

Julian Symons, *The Sunday Times*

"Her best for several books ... a complex double-take plot."
Maurice Richardson, *Observer*

"It is an out-of-the-ordinary story, and one of Miss Bell's best."
"The Greek scene is lovingly described, and the three characters, on holiday from England, are drawn with great care and complete authenticity."

Frances Iles, *The Guardian*
The Sun

THE UPFOLD WITCH

"Josephine Bell makes impressive use of a superstitious village community to conceal her remorseless killer."
The Spectator

"Strongly-plotted mystery ... Detailed and splendidly convincing background of Home Counties village life ... Miss Bell back to her very best form."
Julian Symons, *The Sunday Times*

"It's a good 'un. The villagers sound like villagers and the GP-tec is real."
The Sun

NO ESCAPE

"The whole book shows not only Miss Bell's virtues of sound construction and plotting, but also her engaging readiness to try something new."

Julian Symons, *The Sunday Times*

"Exciting ... readable."

The Observer

"Josephine Bell's excellence in the crime story field is well known. NO ESCAPE will not disappoint her numerous fans."

Aberdeen Press and Journal

DEATH ON THE RESERVE

"Snug read with good topographical detail."

The Observer

"Miss Bell is a bit of a genius at conveying background."

The Sun

"Told in a gossipy style but with excellent engineering."

The Guardian

For regular early information about forthcoming thrillers, send a postcard giving your name and address in block capitals to the The Fiction Editor, Hodder & Stoughton Ltd., St. Paul's House, Warwick Lane, E.C.4